FREAK

FREAK

MARCELLA PIXLEY

**SQUARE
FISH**

FARRAR, STRAUS AND GIROUX

NEW YORK

SQUARE FISH

An Imprint of Macmillan

175 Fifth Avenue

New York, NY 10010

macteenbooks.com

Square Fish books may be purchased for business or promotional use. For information
on bulk purchases, please contact the Macmillan Corporate and Premium Sales Department at
(800) 221-7945 x 5442 or by e-mail at specialmarkets@macmillan.com.

Library of Congress Cataloging-in-Publication Data

Pixley, Marcella Fleischman.

Freak / Marcella Fleischman Pixley

p.   cm.

Summary: Twelve-year-old Miriam, poetic, smart, and quirky, is considered a freak
by the popular girls at her middle school, and she eventually explodes in response
to their bullying, revealing an inner strength she did not know she had.

ISBN 978-1-250-02742-9 (paperback) / ISBN 978-1-4299-3903-4 (e-book)

[1. Identity—Fiction.   2. Bullies—Fiction.   3. Middle schools—Fiction.   4. Schools—
Fiction.   5. Sisters—Fiction.]   I. Title.

PZ7.P68947 Fr 2007   [Fic]—dc22   2006050683

Originally published in the United States by Farrar Straus Giroux
First Square Fish Edition: 2013
Book designed by Barbara Grzeslo
Square Fish logo designed by Filomena Tuosto

10 9 8 7 6 5 4 3 2 1

AR: 5.0 / LEXILE: 750L

To Stephen,
for being my eyes and ears

and

To my students,
for telling their stories and
speaking from the heart

Thanks to the teachers of my childhood who believed I could write, especially Stephanie Diamond, Doug Worth, and George Abbot White. To Esta Markin, who knew how to listen. Thanks to Professor Ken Weedin, who unveiled the glory of words and who inspired this story's beginning, and to Art Smith, who taught me what a poem can do. Thanks to Barbara Lucas for seeing promise in the earliest drafts and to Dixie Goswami and Jackie Jones Royester for daring me to teach what I learned. Much love to my family for believing that this all was possible—I have always stood on their strong shoulders. Finally, I extend my deepest gratitude to my agent, Sally Brady, and my editor, Melanie Kroupa. Their warmth and wisdom pulled me through the final miles of this long journey, and I will never forget their gifts.

FREAK

1

REMEMBER

You do it anyway, even if it hurts,
reach back into the attic,
through the smallest opening,
and you look around in there.
I can remember some things
so clearly, I could trick myself,
imagine that I was falling
all over again. The sound of wings,
of feathered voices, whispering.

Sometimes when you try to make sense of things, they're foggy, and you have to reach way back to pull up the shadows. Even then sometimes they're too dark to really see. Other things are clear as pain, so recent that remembering takes over, and all you can do is sit back and let the memories come. When I try to write down what happened to me, this is what it's like: a symphony blaring all the parts at once, a gigantic puzzle that you have to put back together piece by piece. And all I can do is write it down fast so I only have to do it this once, and then maybe, just maybe, I'll be done with it forever.

If you asked me how the whole mess started, I would tell you it happened around the same time Artie came to stay. Artie's parents had decided to spend their sabbatical in India. They were always saying they wanted to do something good for the world, and suddenly there was this organization that was going to install hot and cold running water in a village somewhere. They asked Artie to come with them, but he wasn't about to spend his senior year digging ditches, for goodness' sake. Artie's father asked my father, and my father asked us. But before we made any decisions, we had a meeting in the living room to discuss whether or not Artie could stay. My parents call these meetings living room democracies. They're essential to our family dynamics. Each member of the family has to vote yes or no.

During living room democracies, I like to sit in the orange armchair and read the *Oxford English Dictionary*. I'm trying to memorize every word in the English language so that one day, when I become poet laureate, I can say it's because of all the words I learned when I was in seventh grade. My mom is proud of my big vocabulary. She says that when God painted me, he spent so much time making me interesting he didn't have the energy left to make me beautiful, but that's fine with her because there are more important things in life than a pretty face. I know I'm nothing like Deborah, who discovered she was beautiful when she was twelve like me. Now that she's a freshman in high school, she seems like a flower when she walks into a room, all fragrant and blooming. It used to be that Deborah would read the *Oxford English Dictionary* with me. We'd make a pillow fort on the living room rug and find all the Latin roots. Deborah used to say them out loud, and I'd write them down in our notebook so we would remember them forever.

Now, my reading the dictionary drives Deborah crazy because it reminds her that she used to be intelligent like me. Deborah says boys are intimidated by women who are cerebral, so I'd better work on my Feminine Attributes, the parts that make boys turn their heads and whistle when you walk by. Deborah has a lot of Feminine Attributes. She wears everything low and tight so no matter where you look, you can see skin. As for me, I like feeling cuddled up in soft cotton. I'll choose a loose flannel shirt with the sleeves rolled up over a skimpy little tank top any day. Mom says it's good that I know how to be comfortable.

That evening, I was reading the *Ss* all alone and I enunciated each word toward Deborah so the sound of them spit out of my mouth. "*Surreptitious, surreptitial, surreptitiously . . .*"

"Very nice," my father chuckled. "Now put your book away for a minute because we have something important to talk about."

My father is what our gym teacher, Mr. Montane, calls a die-hard liberal. Mr. Montane says this like it's a disease. Like your political beliefs can kill you. Being a die-hard liberal means not getting cable television on purpose. It means riding a bike five miles to Kenmore College because there are enough cars on the road already, for goodness' sake. It means being a little shaggier than other fathers. It means National Public Radio and chamber music concerts and a compost heap in the backyard. I pushed the dictionary away with my bare feet and looked at him while he talked. I like to watch his eyes twinkle.

"Okay, girls," my father said. "Your mother and I wanted to include both of you in this decision because it's going to affect us all." He looked straight at us, and I caught a glimpse of what he might be like as an English professor, talking in his soft voice, sipping on his coffee with a book of poetry in one hand. "Sid and Barbara called last night. They told us their application has been accepted. If all goes well, they'll leave for India at the end of the month. Of course they've invited Artie, but it's his senior year, and things are going so well he just doesn't want to go."

Deborah picked up the dictionary and started riffling through pages, but when she caught me watching she put it down.

"You know how important his acting career is to him," my father went on. "He has auditions for NYU in December, and the Shakespeare festival this fall. Sid asked if we would be willing to let him stay here so he could finish his senior year in peace."

"It could be healthy for us," my mother joined in, her voice smoky and tired from too many late nights in her studio trying to get ready for her opening at the Carlton Community Center. It wasn't anything special, but it was the first show she had given in years. My mother says she would have gone to art school if she hadn't had Deborah so early, but sometimes God works in mysterious ways. My mother's paintings are an acquired taste. They are filled with blurred lines and dusty colors. My mother always has paint under her fingernails and her black hair always has hints of color from her work the night before. That day she had a strand of yellow just behind her ear that made it look like she had dipped her hair in mustard.

"I was telling your father last night. It could be good to have another man around here. A little testosterone to balance the energies."

Deborah rolled her eyes. "Oh, I think he'll bring more than a little testosterone. Artie's totally girl crazy these days."

Artie didn't used to be girl crazy. When he was in middle school, he would come over to play chess with me even though I was only eight. He was pretty good at chess, but sometimes his mind would wander and he would lose track of how I was plotting my attacks. Then I'd win. Or maybe he let me win. I was never sure.

"Judy Clarke told me Artie's the hottest guy in the drama club. Even the popular girls are noticing him now," Deborah said.

"Whatever that means," sighed my mother. "The point is, Artie needs a family. We've known him his whole life. I think we should let him stay."

My father held his cup of coffee. With his other hand, he pushed a mop of hair back onto his head. I know my father is going bald, even if he'll never admit it. He's letting the curly hair on the sides of his head grow long so he can brush it over his bald spot. At first you couldn't really tell, and the extra hair just looked like misplaced bangs, but after a few years the bald in the middle got bigger and the hair on the sides got thinner.

My mother licked two of her fingers and smoothed my father's hair. She's always licking her fingers for one reason or another: either to taste a drop of spilled coffee or to twist her paintbrush into a point or to rub a smudge of dirt off my cheek. I hate it when she does that. She'll lick her fingers and then grab me by the arm so I can't get away. Then she'll rub my cheek hard with wet fingers.

There, she always says, *that's better.* There is nothing worse than having your mother's saliva on your face. Except maybe having it in your hair.

My father didn't seem to mind it, though. He stretched his bare feet on the coffee table and offered her a sip of his coffee. It was espresso. It made our living room smell like a bohemian café. My mother wrinkled her nose and waved his hand away.

"Just think of all the good times you girls had whenever we visited Artie's house," my father said. "Think of all the dinners and slide shows."

"And all the memories of Thanksgiving," my mother sighed. Her voice always sounds like it's sighing. All her sentences dip down at the end like they are falling slowly down rabbit holes, trailing away. "Think of that wonderful Thanksgiving a few years ago. Can you remember it, girls? All those candied yams."

I remembered one Thanksgiving, but not because of the candied yams. We were all in elementary school, and Artie showed us real dead monkey skulls and told us this was how we looked on the inside. Deborah thought it was inhumane to dissect monkeys, and I did too. But the dead monkey skulls had jaws that opened and closed. While everyone was eating apple pie, Artie and I brought a couple of skulls to the dinner table and popped them out in front of Deborah while she was chewing. Opening and closing the jaws, we made them say *monkey see, monkey do* . . . until Deborah threw down her fork and marched off, announcing, *Don't be disgusting.* It was wonderful.

"I don't care as long as he doesn't take a long time in the shower or walk around nude," Deborah announced from the carved rocking chair.

Judging from the length of her showers since she started high school, it was hard to imagine that anyone could take longer than Deborah. I started to think of what Artie might look like in the nude, but that made me blush. I picked up a *National Geographic* and flipped through the pages. I stopped for color pictures of Pygmies in skimpy loincloths. I didn't want to contribute to the family meeting. I couldn't possibly be part of this living room democracy. The thought of Artie living in our house for a whole year was too horrible—and too wonderful—to imagine. He was the only high school senior I had ever known.

Artie was old enough to shave and drive a car, and he knew the names of all the *Star Trek* episodes. He could recite Shakespeare with a real British accent. And best of all, he loved poetry. He had books and books of poetry on his bedroom bookshelf. One time when I was a little girl, he let me look at his collection of Dylan Thomas. I sat on his floor for hours and memorized the poems until Mom called and made me come home. *Apple boughs. Lilting house. Dingle starry. Heydays of his eyes.* I still remember how it felt to say those wonderful, delicious words.

"What do you think, Miriam?" my mother asked.

"What?" I looked up from the *National Geographic.*

"What do you think about Artie coming to stay with us for a while?"

My mother and father leaned forward and waited for me to speak.

"I don't care," I said.

"We all have to vote," Deborah told me, her voice irritating and superior. "If we don't all vote then it's only a partial democracy, and any decision is null and void." She leaned forward on the rocking chair so that she was balanced on its wooden tips and I could see down her shirt to her lacy pink bra. The rocking chair creaked under her weight.

I reached over the table and grabbed my father's espresso with both hands. The smell was so strong I almost dropped it onto the rug, but I closed my eyes tight and, taking a deep breath, downed the whole thing.

"Yes!" I cried. "Yes, I think he should definitely stay here!"

"You are such an alien," Deborah said, rolling her eyes.

I picked up the *National Geographic* and pretended to read, but inside, my heart was pounding. Artie Rosenberg was going to move into our house. Artie with his monkey skulls, Artie with his rehearsals and his scripts, Artie with his yellow Volkswagen Bug and his books of poetry, Artie who knew how to swear in Arabic! Artie Rosenberg, in our house, for a whole year. I turned the page of the *National Geographic*. There was a Pygmy man, standing with a spear in his hand. And he wasn't wearing anything. Not even a loincloth.

2

The night before Artie came to stay, my mother sent me and Deborah up to the attic to get his room ready. She wanted us to get rid of all our old playthings so that he wouldn't be tripping over stuffed animals wherever he stepped.

The attic was filled with things we hadn't touched since our fingers were smaller. In the corner was a bucket of dismembered Barbie dolls that Deborah and I used to operate on, amputating their arms and legs, switching their heads, lighting their hair on fire.

There was Deborah's violin in its dusty case, leaning against the closet door. There was the microscope set Mom and Dad gave us one Chanukah, all boxed up. I remembered that winter we spent hours looking at small things. A piece of dust looked like a forest. A grain of salt looked like diamonds. Now I knew if I lifted the lid, I'd see the butterfly wings Deborah brought back from summer camp one year, and the glass slides where we'd smeared drops of our own blood and scrapings from the insides of our cheeks.

Over by the window was where we used to play *Star Trek* with all our stuffed animals. Deborah was the captain and I was the science officer. Back then, when she said, "You're such an alien," it was a compliment.

I picked up the stuffed poodle we used to call Dr. McCoy and held it out to Deborah, making it pant in its deep gravelly voice. "Remember me? Woof! Remember me, Captain Deborah? Woof! Woof!"

Deborah almost smiled.

I brought him over and made him lick her cheek.

She scowled suddenly and pushed my arm away. "Don't do that," she muttered, wiping her cheek as if it had been slobbered on by a real dog.

"But I've been waiting for you, Captain. Woof!"

"Come on, Miriam. Put him away and help me clean up this mess."

I dropped Dr. McCoy in the garbage bag Mom said she'd donate to the Salvation Army as soon as she got a chance. But I knew it would probably sit for another five years in storage, rotting away like the other bags of family throwaways: snowsuits, picture books, school papers, things we were too tired of to look at anymore.

Deborah dumped the microscope and the bucket of *Star Trek* action figures into the garbage bag. She didn't look at any of them.

"Deborah, remember when we used to play up here all the time?"

She nodded silently, and for a second I thought she was my sister again.

"Remember when we were home from school with chicken pox, Mom let us bring our meals up here so she wouldn't have to hear us scratching? Do you remember you were so itchy you paid me a dollar to scratch your back with my fingernails?"

Deborah shook the plastic bag to make more room. "Gross. Why do you keep bringing that up?"

I scooped a handful of clothes and threw them into the bag: old nightgowns, animal slippers, Halloween costumes.

"Remember when we used to tie towels around our necks and run around the house like superheroes?"

"No, I don't remember that," said Deborah, but I knew she was lying.

Deborah put a new sheet and pillowcase on the bed in the corner and went to the closet where Grandma Anne's quilt lay folded and unused. She shook it and the quilt unrolled like a sunset. "Help me do this, Miriam."

I caught my corners at the bottom and we tucked them in, all snug along the sides. "Remember when we used to make forts in the blankets, and we'd go in with our animals and pretend it was another world?"

Deborah turned away.

"Remember you used to bring your violin up here to practice? I loved that. I could hear you practicing in the middle of the night for that concerto competition. I'd hear Vivaldi in my head all night long. *Dum de de dum de de dum.* Do you remember that piece? If I took your violin out of its case and handed it to you, do you think you could still play it? Do you even remember how to hold the bow?"

Deborah sighed like Mom did whenever she was exasperated because I'd been talking too much and she was tired of my noise. "Miriam," she finally said, "it's enough, okay?"

I fluffed up the pillow.

She wiped off the big wooden desk with a damp cloth.

I worked up my courage and turned back to look at her. "Deborah, why don't you want to do things with me anymore?"

Deborah sprayed lemon cleaner on the old oak desk.

"I asked you a question."

She didn't look at me. "Please let's finish this," she said.

I picked up my old scrapbook and started looking through the pages. There was Deborah at seven and me at five. Halloween tigers. Orange crepe-paper ears and black whiskers. *Turn the page.* Another one from the same year. Chanukah. Faces lit by candlelight. The new microscope already opened. *Turn the page.* Deborah at ten and me at eight. The top of Mount Monadnock. Green army canteens and walking sticks. Long braids and red bandannas. Another one from the same year. Sitting in the low branches of Grandpa's maple tree. *Turn the page.* Eleven and nine. Kenmore Music School performance hall. Deborah on violin and me on cello. Serious faces. Music stands. Another one from later that year, cousin Gary's bar mitzvah. Deborah wearing makeup for the first time. She's taller and all of a sudden she has a woman's body. She's grinning and staring right into the camera, but I'm looking somewhere else, my face all wrinkled like I'm smelling rotten eggs. *Turn the page.*

And then, there it is. Deborah's graduation from Carlton Middle School, just last spring. Eighth grade. Sixth grade. Deborah gorgeous in a white strapless sundress. Me in jogging shorts and a T-shirt with an iron-on decal of a flying unicorn. Neither of us smiling. Each of us looking in separate directions.

Deborah picked up the scrapbook and put it face down in the top drawer.

"Deborah," I said.

"Miriam, I don't want to talk about this." She sprayed more lemon cleaner and scrubbed and scrubbed and scrubbed.

"Deborah," I said again.

I took the cleaning spray out of her hand and stood in front of her so she had to look at me. For just a moment, her eyes met my eyes.

"I don't want to talk about this," Deborah said again. "Please stop trying to make me explain something that doesn't have an explanation."

"There has to be an explanation."

Deborah opened her mouth and then closed it again like a fish trapped behind glass. Then she took a breath. "It's not that you did something wrong, Miriam. I just got sick of everyone thinking I was some kind of freak. Kids like me now. Do you know what a big deal that is? Kids don't think I'm weird."

"It's good to be weird. Who cares if people think you're weird?"

"I do," Deborah told me, her voice tight and pained. "I know you don't care what other people think of you, and that's okay. But I care, Miriam. You have to understand this. I like having friends. I like being invited to parties. For the first time in my life, people think I'm the same as everyone else. I'm not going to do anything to mess that up."

Tears welled up in my eyes, but I didn't want Deborah to see me cry like a baby, so I turned my face and wiped my hands over the quilt, smoothing out wrinkles that weren't there.

"And while we're on the topic," Deborah went on breathlessly, her voice propelled by the momentum of truths tumbling into the room, "I wish you would remember how I feel about this when Artie's around. Try not to embarrass me. Try not to talk his ear off. Try not to bring up all the weird things we did as kids."

I traced the pattern of flowers with my finger, the curved line of roses and daisies. When I was a very little girl, this used to be my favorite quilt. I used to make myself feel better by holding a corner of it between my thumb and two fingers and rubbing it against the side of my face. It was like a rabbit ear. Like the inside of the softest rabbit ear. Now something inside me wanted to pick it up and hold it to my cheek and cry, but I didn't. I just touched the pattern and tried not to let Deborah see my face.

"I hate you," I whispered so softly the words were almost not even there.

"What was that?"

"Nothing," I said. "Let's just finish this. I want Artie to love this room."

I sifted through our stuffed animals. Then I closed my eyes and touched each one on the head before throwing it away.

3

MORNING SONG

The way it must have been
on that first early morning,
light just starting to wake,
gardens, apples brimming.

The morning before Artie moved in, I wrote in Clyde. Clyde was my journal. I know most people don't give their journals names, but most people never had a journal like Clyde. Clyde was much more than a spiral notebook with a torn cover and pages falling out. He was the place I wrote all my poems and problems so one day I could look back and say, *It's all right, Miriam. It all turned out all right anyhow.*

Dear Clyde,

It's so early in the morning the sun hasn't even woken up. The world is still cast in a gray shadow, but I can't sleep another moment.

Last night I kept on waking to check my alarm clock and count how many seconds were left until today.

Artie's the one person in this world who really understands me. He's going to wake up my poetry. He's going to give me something to really write about. And it all starts today. Today is a scrumptiously serendipitous day. Today is even better than a birthday.

It's six in the morning. The sun unfolds its rays behind my window blinds like a fan opening up rib by rib. I'm going to use Deborah's kiwi shampoo for extra shine. I'm going to put perfume under my armpits. From now on, I am going to be ravishing. Six in the morning. 24,000 seconds until Artie comes to stay.

Signing off,
Miriam Fisher, Esquire

I've never had very many friends. I don't think there's anything wrong with me, per se. I don't smell bad. I don't sit in the corner and talk to my fingers like Bonnie Trotsky, who has to go upstairs to Dr. Rudder's room three times a week. I think it has more to do with the other kids in our neighborhood. They just aren't interested in things the way I am. Here's an example. They like parties. I like poetry. They like brushing their hair. I like looking at my hair under a microscope. You get the picture.

Ever since Deborah started high school, I've been hanging out with Rosie Baker. She's not as good a friend as Deborah was, but we have fun telling secrets and hiding from the popular girls. Rosie's funny and smarter than most of the kids at Carlton Middle School. She doesn't care that her clothes are the wrong brand or that her hair is so curly it makes her head look like a bird's nest.

She gets good grades like I do. Plus she's got an attitude. She's smoked a cigarette, she knows how to make food come out of her nose when she laughs, and she says she once French-kissed Marco Yerardi for thirty-nine and a half minutes out behind the gym. I don't believe the part about the kiss, but I like to ask her for details to see how good she is at making stuff up.

The day that Artie came to stay, Rosie and I walked past the American flag hanging by the lockers. We walked past the Founding Fathers bulletin board covered with posters of George Washington, John Hancock, and Thomas Jefferson. We walked past the sign-up sheets for the Carlton soccer team and the sickly sweet inspirational posters with sayings like *Go the Distance* and *Reach for the Stars* and other totally obvious things designed to make us want to try harder.

The popular girls were gathered in a tight circle by the lockers. There was a buzz of activity around them. In the center of the circle stood Misty Marin, who always looks like she's frowning even when she smiles. There was Tracy Blair with her blond ponytail. And then there was Jenny Clarke, who is the prettiest girl in the seventh grade because she has boobs like a grownup woman. Jenny was held back last year, so she's a full year older than the rest of us. She always wears miniskirts and low-cut tank tops, and her legs and arms are so skinny you can see the outline of her bones. Every time Misty laughed, Jenny laughed too.

I couldn't tell what the popular girls were talking about. All I could see was a hive of perfect bodies packed into blue jeans. They leaned. They shifted. They flipped their hair when they laughed. They created a zone of perfume, so when we walked by it was like passing an exploded watermelon that someone had dropped on a city street in August: *so* pungent you might die if you stopped and breathed its scent long enough.

"Hey, Rosie," I said, "I want to tell you something."

"Fire away, Shakespeare," Rosie answered.

Rosie's the one who started calling me Shakespeare and then it kind of stuck. I think it's because in fifth grade I showed her a poem I wrote and she was really impressed. That morning Rosie was wearing her father's black leather vest. She had drawn leaves and swirls all over her hands with black magic marker so it looked like she was wearing lace gloves. One thing you can say about Rosie Baker: she dares to be different. And that's not such an easy thing in Carlton.

"Artie Rosenberg's coming to live at my house."

"You lie." Rosie stared at me from behind the red bird's nest of her hair. Rosie's hair is so unruly she looks like she's been raised by wolves. It's curlier than curly and even when she spits in her palm and wets it down, it springs out again like some kind of wild animal on her head. She doesn't care. Rosie says having curly hair is sort of like having a pet.

"No. It's true. He's coming this afternoon and he'll be with us the rest of the school year."

Rosie opened her mouth, but no sound came out. I guess you could say that she was flabbergasted. I like saying that—*flabbergasted*. The *Compact Edition of the Oxford English Dictionary* says that *flabbergast* means "to put a person in such confusion that he does not know what to say." Rosie Baker is almost never flabbergasted.

I went on. Talking about Artie made me feel flushed and happy

20

and breathless all at once. "Artie is the perfect boy. I'm telling you. He's smart. He's talented. He's funny. He loves poetry. I think this is meant to be. I can feel it."

Rosie looked like she was going to spontaneously combust, her hair springing around her face like snakes. She clutched my hand. "I've always had a huge crush on him," she breathed.

"Me too," I said. "Ever since I was little. Rosie, I wouldn't be saying this if I didn't mean it, but I think Artie Rosenberg could be my soul mate. I think maybe he's The One."

Rosie leaned in and grabbed my hands. Her face was so close to mine that I could smell the crab salad in her braces. "My sister got to kiss him onstage," she whispered. "She says he knows how to do things with his tongue that I can't even say in public. He invented a kind of French kiss called The Flutter where he moves his tongue up and down so fast it feels like your whole mouth is vibrating. My sister says that when she was Juliet they did The Flutter for fifteen and a half seconds and when it was over she could barely say her lines."

"I wish he would do that to me," I sighed, clutching Rosie's hands. "Rosie. Be honest. Do you think someone like Artie would ever want to kiss someone like me?"

Rosie squawked like a huge red bird and then nearly fell down trying to stop herself from laughing. "Oh, my good lord!" she sputtered. "I can just see it. It'll be Miriam Fisher and Artie Rosenberg, fluttering away tonight, baby! Rolling like wolverines in the autumn leaves."

I grinned and clamped my hand over her mouth but she pushed it away and went on.

"Honey, you'll come back to school tomorrow with the blush of love on your cheeks and maple leaves in your hair. I can see it now! Oh, Artie, put your tongue in my mouth and flutter me, baby." Rosie embraced herself and started making strange gargling noises.

"Rosie, stop it," I hissed. She was getting louder and a few of the popular girls had turned to stare. I clamped my hand over her mouth again, but she laughed so hard that spit sluiced onto my palm. I wiped my hand on my jeans.

"Hold me, baby! I've always loved you! Even before you were Romeo. Forsooth! Oh, Artie! Oh, Miriam!" Rosie tried to do The Flutter inside her own mouth. She almost fell down laughing.

That's when I noticed Jenny Clarke breaking from the circle of popular girls and walking over to us. The popular girls watched her, their bodies even closer together than they were before.

"Hey, Miriam," said Jenny, "why don't you and Rosie flutter each other?"

The watermelon girls giggled.

"That's mean," I said.

Jenny Clarke brushed a strand of my hair back behind my ear. Then she reached in her backpack and handed me a piece of gum. "I'm just kidding," she said. "Can't you take a joke?"

"Of course I can take a joke," I told her.

"Good. 'Cause I have a really good one for you. What girl in the seventh grade is so flat she looks like a boy?"

I held my breath.

Jenny reached out and grabbed my shirt. She pulled down the collar. I could feel cold air on my chest. Jenny Clarke stared down my front as if she was looking for something. Then she turned back to the popular girls with a huge, white smile on her face. "Oh! Wait a minute!" Jenny shrieked. "She *is* a boy."

Misty Marin and Tracy Blair burst out laughing.

I sort of smiled like I was with them, but smiling made it seem like I liked having Jenny look down my shirt, which I didn't. I wanted to push her away. I wanted to grab her wrists and throw her against the lockers, but I couldn't move. All their eyes were on me and they were all smiling, and even though they were down the hall, for a moment it seemed as though I was surrounded by watermelon lip gloss and mouths filled with straight teeth.

Jenny leaned close to my face. "Do you really think Artie Rosenberg would want to kiss someone like you?"

I couldn't speak. I was frozen.

"Well, I've got news for you. Artie Rosenberg only likes real girls. He wouldn't even notice someone who looked like you."

Jenny pushed my flat chest with both her hands. I stumbled and fell backward into the lockers. And then everyone laughed. Even me.

The third period bell rang. Misty Marin and Tracy Blair shouldered their backpacks, took each other's arms, and hurried away toward the science lab, their high-heeled boots clattering down the corridor. None of them said anything to Jenny or to me. Jenny watched until they disappeared around the corner.

Miss Garland opened the door to her classroom and stuck out her head. She saw me crouching on the floor. She saw Jenny Clarke standing over me. She stepped into the hall and put her hands on her hips. "Hey, what's going on out here?"

"Nothing," I said.

"Nothing," said Jenny Clarke. She pulled me up and put her skinny arm around my shoulders. "We were just going to class."

"We don't want to be late," said Rosie Baker. "We have a test."

"Are you okay, Miriam?" Miss Garland asked.

Jenny's arm tightened around my shoulders.

"I'm fine," I told her, "just fine."

4

The only place on earth I hate as much as the lockers is the school bus. The school bus is a physical map of who's cool and who isn't. No one tells you where to sit. There isn't any seating chart. But if you know who you are, you know where to go. Here's how it works: the more popular you are, the closer you sit to the back of the bus; the more of a loser you are, the closer you sit to the front. It's as easy as that. In the back, the kids vandalize seat covers, make out, pass notes, and throw spit wads at the front of the bus; in the front of the bus, kids read, do homework, look out the window, and try to disappear. Kids at the back of the bus are beautiful. They find each other because being seen together makes them look even better. Kids at the front of the bus know they are defective. They have pimples or glasses or crooked teeth or greasy hair. They are embarrassed to be seen.

The only thing more dangerous than being a loser with a group of popular kids behind you is being part of a group of losers all corralled together, like pathetic lambs waiting to be slaughtered.

And here's the worst part. We hate each other. We hate each other even more than the popular kids hate us. We hate each other because when we look at each other, we can see what they are laughing at.

I pushed my way through the doors and let my feet carry me down the aisle. The first rows of seats were already taken. That's where I like to sit. Right in front. That way there is a buffer of three or four rows separating me from the popular kids in the back. Back and back I went. Past Kenny Bernard, who was already doing his homework. Past Ralph Mangan and Pamela Drum, who were wearing *Star Trek* pins and looking at the green vinyl seat cushions with the magnifying glass they had stolen from the science lab. Past the exchange students, who talked to each other in languages no one could understand and who wore clothes that had strange slogans in mock-English: *Thunder College*, *Shark Boys*, *Cutie Peach*, things that didn't translate. As I walked back, the other losers turned their faces away.

There was one seat open next to Mary Barnes, who was only a loser because she was fat. I squeezed in. The bus pulled out and rounded the traffic circle. I felt Mary Barnes's arm push against my side because the seat was too small for both of us. I gave a weak smile, sort of apologizing for our predicament, but she turned her face and stared out the window as if Old Forge Road was the most interesting thing in the world. I watched her watch the factory buildings go by.

Suddenly, there was a commotion behind me. The popular girls were laughing.

"Kiss her on the mouth," Misty Marin was saying. "I dare you."

"Give her a hickey."

I turned around in my seat and raised myself up so I could see. Freddie Harlan was sitting next to Jenny in the back of the bus. He had one arm around her shoulders and the other resting on her bare knee.

Tracy Blair twirled her blond ponytail with one finger. "She'll let you do anything. Won't you, Jenny?"

Jenny Clarke pushed his hand away. "Maybe."

"I bet you won't let him give you a hickey."

"Yeah, I would."

Jenny flashed a white smile to Tracy Blair. Then she leaned back so her neck was exposed. For ten whole seconds, all I could see was the back of Freddie Harlan's head. The popular girls cheered him on. Then it was done. When he came away, there was a bright red hickey on the side of Jenny's neck the size of a thumbprint.

"Oh my God, Jenny. You're such a slut," squealed Tracy Blair.

"No, I'm not," Jenny said.

"You let him do it."

"So what? That doesn't make me a slut." Then Jenny spotted me. "What are you staring at?"

"Nothing," I whispered.

"You're such a freak, Miriam Fisher. Turn around and mind your own business."

The popular girls laughed. Jenny took Freddie Harlan's hand and put it back on her knee.

The streets of Carlton went by outside the bus windows: brick buildings and secondhand shops. Kenny Bernard got off. Then Pamela Drum got off. Then the exchange students. We passed empty gasoline stations, vacant lots, and boarded-up houses. When it was time for Jenny Clarke to leave the bus, she pulled herself away from Freddie Harlan and made her way down the aisle, grabbing onto the tops of the seats with both hands. Everyone watched her. One boy made a meowing sound like a cat in heat. The entire bus erupted into laughter. Jenny stopped at my seat. She looked me straight in the eyes. For a moment it looked like she was going to say something. Then she shoved me so hard that I fell into Mary Barnes.

Jenny stomped down the bus steps and onto her street. Someone had thrown an empty cigarette pack onto the flagstones. She kicked it out of the way and climbed up the porch stairs. There was a rusty bicycle and a pile of old wooden crates stacked next to the door. She took a key from around her neck and let herself in. The screen door slammed behind her.

5

The bus drove past St. Peter's Lodge and then past the highway that goes out of town to Kenmore College where my father and Artie's father teach English. When I got off the bus at Mill Street, I could see Artie's ancient yellow Volkswagen convertible parked right outside my house. One of the front wheels was up on the curb, and the end of the car jutted out into the road. The back window had a translucent decal of a unicorn with rainbows and butterflies coming out of its mane. The fender had a bumper sticker that said *The Pen Is Mightier than the Sword.*

I walked around to the driver's side and looked at myself in the side mirror. I was a mess. My hair was greasy. There was a pimple on my forehead the size of a gumdrop. I parted my hair on the side, and tossed my mousy bangs across my forehead. With the pimple covered, I almost looked okay. I pinched my cheeks until they were bright red, and unbuttoned the first two buttons of my shirt. There. Now I almost looked pretty.

Deborah and Artie were already sitting at the kitchen table.

Artie was even more handsome than I remembered. Deborah was right. All those school plays must have changed him. Where he used to be lanky, all long arms and legs that seemed to get in the way of the rest of his body, there were muscles. His T-shirt was stretched tight across his chest. When he moved his arm to take a glass of milk, I could see the back of his wrist. It was covered by man hair. I had seen his wrists plenty of times playing chess, but they had never made me feel like this.

"*Hola*, Shakespeare," said Artie.

I brushed my bangs back with my fingers. "*Hola, Arturo. ¿Como esta?*"

I plunked myself down at the kitchen table between Artie and my sister. My mother suddenly emerged from the pantry with a plate filled with odds and ends. She had smudges of blue and gray paint across her cheek, which meant she had been working on a painting she calls *Child in the Rain*. *Child in the Rain* was the closest thing she had to a masterpiece. I didn't just think this because it happened to be her one and only painting of me. There was something special about it. Something about the little girl, about the way the rain came down on her hands, that made me want to stand and look at it for hours.

My mother laid the food on the kitchen table and then left to go back to her painting. There were pickles from the deli, cans of sardines and herring, a plastic container of tabouli and another one filled with garlic hummus. There were sliced cucumbers and tomatoes from the garden and an assortment of sandwiches all cut into perfect finger-sized triangles with the crusts cut off, the way I liked them best. Artie reached across the table and took three. I took three too. I bit into mine when he bit into his and I tried to time it so I chewed exactly when he chewed. His jaw, my jaw. His teeth, my teeth. His tongue, my tongue.

I took a deep breath. I was ready to make an unforgettable impression. "I knew you were here when the bus let me off," I told Artie. "I saw your car. It's such a nice car. I mean it's interesting. A lot of guys your age, they just have any old car. They don't do anything to make it unique. But your car is definitely the most unique car I've ever seen. It's an expression of your creativity. I'd love a car like that. Oh, I know I'm too young to drive, but someday, when I'm sixteen, I'd like to drive a car just like yours, Artie."

We chewed our sandwiches and swallowed.

"Do you like tuna fish?" I asked him. "I like it too, I guess. But you never really know what you're getting into with tuna. You have to be careful, because Miss Garland says tuna like to swim underneath dolphins, did you know that? They swim right underneath, so when the fishermen set traps for the tuna, they end up catching the dolphins too. And it's worse killing a dolphin. Dolphins are mammals. They nurse their young just like people do."

"Pigs nurse their young," said Artie. He bit into a ham sandwich. Deborah laughed a fake laugh as if this was the best joke she had ever heard.

"But pigs aren't as smart as dolphins. Except Wilbur, I guess. Do you know who I mean when I say *Wilbur*?"

There was no answer, so I went on.

"Wilbur is the pig in *Charlotte's Web*. He's a pretty smart pig. I mean he can talk and everything, and I've never read about a dolphin who could do that. Except I guess Wilbur doesn't really count, because he's just a storybook pig and he's really meant for younger kids who don't know any better, especially when it comes to the intellectual abilities of pigs. But you never know with fiction. I mean, it has to come from somewhere, doesn't it? Somewhere in the writer's life there could have been a pig called Wilbur who could talk and talk and talk, better than any old dolphin, or person even."

Artie smiled at me and wiped his lips with a napkin. "Or you," he said.

"Or me." I wiped my lips too. It was heavenly. "But you know, Artie, eventually we all end up dead. I mean, statistically speaking, the odds are one to one. We all die of something. Maybe not now, but eventually. It's the fate of humanity. Which brings us back to *Charlotte's Web*. Even though it's fiction and is meant for younger kids, the author isn't afraid to tell the truth, and that's why it's such a good book. I mean, Charlotte dies, Artie. Charlotte the spider knows that she is mortal and by the end of the novel she just up and dies. But it's what she does when she's alive that is so important. I mean, she saves Wilbur's life. Do you know what I'm saying?"

"Absolutely." Artie chuckled, his mouth filled with ham.

"Did you know that when Deborah and I were little kids the ending of *Charlotte's Web* always used to make Deborah weep? I mean really *weep*—with sound coming out and snot and tears and everything. Every time we read it, you'd think it was a family member who had died and not a fictional spider. Deborah's always been sensitive like that. I bet you can't tell it by looking at her, but she is. She's a regular bleeding heart." I put my hand on Deborah's hand across the table.

"For crying out loud, Miriam," Deborah said, pulling away. "You don't have to bore him to death his first day here. Just ignore her, Artie. Sometimes she just talks to hear the sound of her own voice."

Artie smiled. "She could never bore me. We're kindred spirits, right, Shakespeare? Two peas in a pod. Come over here, you." Artie reached over and gave me a giant noogie, putting one arm around my shoulders and the other one on the top of my head. He scruffled up my hair and I could feel myself beaming as I wriggled free. He was wonderful. He was even more wonderful than I had imagined. I noogied him back and then Artie tickled my knees until I scrunched back into my chair and held myself and laughed.

"Hey," said Artie, suddenly remembering, "do you still play chess?"

I grinned. "Of course I do. And I'm even better than I used to be, so watch out."

"Oh, no," said Artie. "It's you who should watch out. I may not be a chess club nerd anymore, but I'm still pretty darned good. It's very unlikely that you will ever beat me, no matter how smart you are. So be on thy watch, young Miriam, or I shall slayest thee."

"Ho-ho!" I said, raising my arm like I was brandishing a sword. "Hey, Artie. Do you remember that one game that went on for seven hours? I was so tired at the end I thought my brain was going to implode. Do you think that's possible? Do you think a brain could work so hard that it could short-circuit and become nothing but a quivering mass of jelly?"

"Not *your* brain." Artie laughed. "Not a chance. Of course I remember that game. That was the best game of chess I ever played in my life. Even though it was against an eight-year-old."

"I'm so glad you're here, Artie," I said. And I meant it.

Deborah stared at us. Then she dipped her pinky finger into the hummus and licked it off. She did it again. Lick. Swallow. Lick. Swallow. Artie couldn't stop looking at her.

"Hey, Miriam," she said. "I have an idea. Maybe after chess, you can show Artie that bag of stuffed animals. Miriam has a great imagination, Artie. Last night, all she wanted to do was sit on the floor and play with her stuffed animals. Why don't you show Artie that doggie. What's his name? Dr. McCoy? He's your favorite, isn't he?"

"No," I said, unsure where this was heading.

"Yes, he is," Deborah insisted. "Don't you remember? You told me last night how you couldn't wait for Artie to come because you thought maybe he would want to play animals with you. Didn't you tell me that?"

"No," I said.

"Oh, yes you did." Deborah smiled. "But don't worry, Artie. Miriam's really good at amusing herself without anyone else around." Deborah reached out and gave me a little hug like I was a five-year-old. It was the first time she had touched me in a year. "They grow up so fast, don't they?" She smiled the sweetest, most beautiful smile, and threw back her long black hair. Artie smiled right back at her.

I felt the blood rising to my cheeks. "I have to go to the bathroom," I said.

I ran upstairs and stared at myself in the mirror. Jenny Clarke was right. I didn't look like a girl at all. I looked more like a gargoyle, all angles and corners, nothing soft, nothing nice to look at. The pimple reared its ugly head through the curtain of my hair. I put my thumb and forefinger on either side of it and squeezed and squeezed until it erupted red and white against the bathroom mirror.

6

TURKEY AIR

Something happens to my nostrils
when I am breathing turkey air.
They open wide as a barn door,
the hairs on the inside, twitching,
the wet, nosey caverns, pink
to the smell. The skin plumps.
Downstairs, the kitchen windows
perspire. The scent glazes each pane.
If I could plan my death, turkey air
would be my last humming breath.

It's hard to stay upset when my dad is cooking turkey. On Fridays he finishes teaching early, so sometimes he makes a special dinner for the whole family. In the fall, my dad likes to drive out to McEwen's Farm and pick out a big fat organic turkey. He brings it home, stuffs it with bread crumbs and onions, and covers it with tinfoil so the juice stays inside but the skin gets all golden and crispy. The night Artie came to stay, he sang to the turkey as it roasted inside our oven. *Marvelous bird.* I could hear his scratchy tenor voice. *Wonderful bird, heavenly bird.*

And it did smell heavenly. The smell of turkey roasting, of potatoes and onions and gravy, spread through the kitchen, up the stairs, and into every corner of the house. Lying on the bed in my room, I breathed in turkey air and felt better. I opened Clyde to the next clean page.

Dear Clyde,

Sometimes I wonder if there is such a thing as God. Why would there be people in this world as mean as Jenny Clarke, and why would there be sisters who suddenly realize they are beautiful, and then turn their backs, and why would God make adults if none of them ever notice when something is going wrong?

But then I take a breath of my father's roast turkey and I realize that smells can be heavenly. Maybe roast turkey is the proof of God's existence. The Oxford English Dictionary *says that* heavenly *means "having the excellence, beauty, or delight that belongs to heaven; of more than earthly or human excellence; divine."*

Maybe my father's turkey is divine. Maybe it will save me from this horrible day. O Turkey roasting down there all full of carrots and potatoes. O excellent, beautiful, delightful Turkey. Erase this horrible day and make everything right again.

My father is singing turkey songs downstairs. His voice is so beau-

*tiful—and low and lilting. If I close my eyes and listen, it almost
sounds like a prayer.*

Signing off,
Miriam Fisher, Esquire

"Hey, Miriam," my father called up the stairs in a voice loud enough to fill a lecture hall. "We're waiting for you. What are you writing, an epic poem?"

"Pulitzer Prize," I shouted back down the stairs. I slammed Clyde's cover and carried him over to his hiding place.

One of the good things about living in an old house is that there are all sorts of nooks and crannies, perfect for hiding things. Carlton used to be a boomtown before the railroads closed. All the houses up and down our street were built for the workers. They aren't beautiful, but they are solid and they still have remains of the past inside them. Instead of stand-up radiators, our house has cast-iron heating vents. The one in my bedroom provides a perfect hiding place for Clyde because you can lift the grating up and there is a big empty space in the floor just the right size. I curled my fingers into the grating, and lowered Clyde down.

"Miriam. Let's go," called Deborah up the stairs. "We're all waiting for you."

The table was set for guests. When it's just our family we take for ourselves: whatever plate, whatever cup, whatever silverware. Sometimes we use napkins, sometimes we don't. But it's different when someone comes over. In my mom's family, they all used to get together on Fridays and everyone would bring something.

Aunt Lillian would bring pickled herring, and Aunt Bess would cook a Kosher chicken. There would be challah and matzoh ball soup and wine and they would use real silver and plates that matched. My mother told me the stories so many times, I could almost smell the onions and chicken fat all these years later and all these miles from Brooklyn. I could almost hear them all talking at once, arguing politics and religion and art.

I pulled a chair between Artie and Deborah and put my napkin on my lap.

"*Hola*, Shakespeare," said Artie.

My father took the turkey out of the oven and set it at the center of the table. It was beautiful. Brown and crispy. Just the way I loved it. The scent of it warmed the room and glazed the kitchen windows with steam. He carved white meat and dark meat, breaking off the drumsticks and wings. "Take whatever you want, everybody," he announced.

My mother passed around the plates. You could see remnants of *Child in the Rain* on her hands. The grays and blues made her knuckles look bruised. "Oh lord, my hands." She smiled apologetically, but it wasn't really a smile. "Occupational hazard. Don't worry. None of it came off on the food."

My father heaped turkey onto his plate. "There's more than enough for everyone to have seconds and thirds and so on. Artie, can I offer you white or dark?"

"Dark, please," Artie said, holding out his plate. "This looks delicious, Mr. Fisher. A feast for kings."

My mother smiled and poured wine into his glass. "This is mead," she told him. "It's made from fermented honey. You'll love this, Artie. It was popular in Renaissance England. Take a sip. It's warm and golden." My mother was always using colors in sentences where they didn't really belong, but I liked the sound of her words. *Warm and golden. Warm and golden.* That would be good in a poem. I scribbled it down on my napkin.

"So, Artie," said my father, breaking the silence, "what play are you working on these days?"

"We just started *Hamlet*."

"Ah! One of the best!" said my father. "You know, Doris did some acting in college. She was a perfect Ophelia. Gloomy and melodramatic. 'O, what a noble mind is here o'erthrown!' You're Hamlet, I assume."

Artie smiled and rolled his hand in the air like he was bowing with a feathered hat.

"How's it going?"

"It's a challenge. But I like it." Artie took a sip of mead.

I imagined how the inside of his mouth must have tasted right at that moment. Warm and golden. I raised my wineglass to my nose and breathed in as deeply as I could. The beginnings of a poem came all at once. "*Warm and golden, warm and golden, the smell of summer sunsets 'cross dusty city streets . . .*" I whispered.

"What's wrong with you?" said Deborah.

"Shhhh," I said, "I'm writing a poem."

"Miriam's a bit of an actress herself," explained my mother.

"Yes, she is." Artie smiled. "I've always known that."

I grinned back at him. It pays to be a poet.

"There are two kinds of people in this world," my father intoned with sparkling eyes. "Those who like to be in the spotlight, and those who despise it."

"Marty's an extrovert," my mother said. "Put him in a lecture hall and he comes alive. I'm the opposite. I need time alone. The girls aren't allowed to speak to me before I've had my coffee in the morning. I know they resent it, but I do better work if I start my day in silence."

"So how are your paintings going, Mrs. Fisher?" Artie asked.

"Terrible." My mother grinned despite herself. Then, "Did the girls tell you? I have an opening at the Community Center next week. It's the first show I've had in years." She sighed. "I envy your youth, Artie. You have everything ahead of you. You know, I would have gone on to graduate school if I hadn't had Deborah so young."

Deborah frowned down at her plate.

"But things are certainly going well for you, Artie," my father said. "Seems like we're hearing your name everywhere these days. Front page of the *Carlton Tribune*. Honor Roll. Lead in the school play. So, here's the big question. Has all the recognition changed you, or are you still the same kid who used to stumble in here with a chessboard under his arm?"

"I don't know if I've changed all that much," Artie said, coloring a little.

"Oh, you've changed. No question." My mother laughed. "Look at you. You're so handsome and confident. All that awkwardness is gone. Poof!"

"I guess it's from being onstage so much," Artie said. "You can't be awkward when people are looking at you. You have to reach inside yourself and find your inner strength."

My mother put down her fork. "You're so articulate. Isn't he articulate, Marty? 'You have to reach inside yourself and find your inner strength.' Isn't that the truth. Especially when so many teenagers give up on their gifts in order to fit in."

Artie took another sip of mead. He licked the rim of his glass.

I waved my fork in the air. *"Warm and golden like honey on the tongue, the smell of summer sunsets!"* I had finally gotten the words just right. Now all I had to do was remember them long enough to write them down on my napkin.

"Spotlight!" My father waved his hands like he was casting a spell. "The young girl recites poetry. We look at her. All the world's a stage. And in that moment, she becomes the actor and we become the audience. Applause, applause. But not everybody wants the spotlight. For instance, Deborah here has decided she will never set foot on a stage again. She has given up violin and now all she does is talk on the telephone."

"Please," said Deborah, seething, "let's not go over this again."

"Artie is trying to fulfill his potential," my mother snapped. "Your father and I think it's commendable. Don't you think it's commendable, Deborah?"

"Sure," muttered Deborah. "It's commendable."

I put my hand on Deborah's elbow. *"Commendable. Adjective. Deserving of praise. Laudable."*

"Shut up, Miriam," Deborah hissed.

"Contrary to what she might tell you, Deborah is a very talented musician," my father told Artie. "She has recently quit violin after ten years of lessons. Now she doesn't even practice."

"It's not her fault," I quickly offered. "She just has too much homework."

My mother pointed to Deborah with her fork. "If she did any

homework at all I'd be happy. But she's on the phone with that Judy Clarke until all hours of the night. Then she brings home a seventy-five on one math test and a seventy-three on another and she tells me I should be happy because most of her friends failed. Tell me, Artie. Should I be happy about this?"

"Most of her friends will get married before they turn twenty," my father said without missing a beat. "They'll stay in Carlton their whole lives. They'll end up working in the same factories where their mothers worked."

"If you hate this town so much, why did we move here?" Deborah muttered.

"It's what we could afford," my mother said, her mouth in a tight little smile.

"I don't think Carlton is so bad," Artie told us. "Just because a lot of people are poor doesn't mean they aren't smart."

"Oh, Artie. I know that," my father said.

"Deborah's Grandpa was a factory worker," my mother told Artie. "He never graduated from high school. He worked until the day he died. All he wanted was to see us happy."

Deborah glared at her. "And are you happy, Mother?"

My mother cut herself a piece of turkey. Her hands shook.

My father reached out and steadied her. "Grandpa would be proud of you," he told her in a voice so soft he could have been talking to a child. "We've raised two beautiful girls. And we've given them everything they need to make something of themselves. Deborah may be hiding her talents, Doris, but Miriam is still striving to be extraordinary. She's going to get there. One way or another, Doris, Miriam will get there."

My mother nodded and tried to smile. She looked over at me.

Then she touched the side of my face with her hand. When she talked again, her voice sounded far away. "Miriam's always been special," my mother whispered, in a flat voice like she was reciting lines from a play. "And people respect her, don't they? People have always respected Miriam."

"I can't believe this," spat Deborah. "You think people respect Miriam? Have you talked to her lately, Mother? Do you know how miserable she is?"

My mother gazed at the pressed tin ceiling as if she were memorizing the patterns, as if she were trying to disappear into the sky like a balloon going farther and farther away. "I don't know what you're talking about, Deborah," she said in a voice as thin as air. "Miriam has always been happy."

Deborah slammed the table with both her hands. "Tell them the truth, Miriam. I was at Judy Clarke's house today. Jenny was there. She told me all about how things are for you at school. Tell Mom how it is during recess. When you walk past your locker. When you pass from one class to the next. Tell her."

My mother looked at me with tired eyes. "What is it you wanted to tell me?" she breathed. The whole table was silent.

"Nothing," I told her. "Everything is absolutely fine."

"That's my girl," my mother whispered, closing her eyes.

7

When dinner was over and the dishes were cleared, Artie and my parents brought espresso into the living room. It was wonderful to hear Artie tell about his plans to audition for theater companies in New York, how he dreamed of being on Broadway. But after a couple of hours I started to get drowsy. Their syllables blurred into each other. The vowels became muddy and muffled, and I knew it was time for me to excuse myself. Even from the bathroom upstairs, I could hear them laughing. Every now and then, my mother's dusky voice rose up through the spaces in the vent, and Artie's low tones were unmistakable through the floorboards, low and velvety as a cello. I could listen to him forever, which is a good thing because it takes nearly that long to clean my pimples.

Cleaning my pimples is an act of pure will. There is an order and a purpose to everything. If you walked in on me, you might think I was conducting some kind of secret ritual. First I take my glasses off and run the hot water into the sink until it's steamy. Then I open the blue bottle of anti-pimple cream and scoop a dollop into each hand. I massage it in one hundred smeary circles all over my face. Forehead, nose, cheeks, and chin . . . forehead, nose, cheeks, and chin . . . I had to be beautiful for Artie. I rubbed my face in circles around and around and around and thought of Artie's cello-y voice talking to me, saying my whole name, not "Shakespeare," or "Kid," but "Miriam," drinking down every syllable so that it sounded like a lullaby, *"Miiiriiiaaam,"* just like that.

I practiced before the mirror. I was Artie singing my name to myself.

"Miiirriiiaaam . . . Miiirriiiaaam."

And then I was me. *"I love the way you sing my name, Arthur."*

And then I was Artie. *"Oh my darling, Miriam, you are the most creative woman I've ever met."*

And then I was me. *"Oh, Arthur, I have been waiting for you to say that my whole life. Oh, Arthur, you make me so happy. I am ready to give myself to your fluttering tongue."*

And then I was Artie. *"Kiss me, you vixen!"*

And then I leaned toward the mirror, my white creamy faces coming close to each other. I turned my head to the side so my noses wouldn't bump, and drawing in a breath as if to take an enormous sip of something delicious, I kissed myself.

"Oh my God. You are so weird."

When I opened my eyes there was a white smeary mess on the bathroom mirror and the hazy reflection of Deborah standing behind me in her lavender bathrobe, arms crossed, long black hair falling over her shoulders.

She sat down on the edge of the bathtub. Her eyes were red and her face was blotchy and I could tell she had been crying. She watched me rub the face cream off the mirror with my sleeve. Her hands were clasped together and she kept wringing her fingers. I wanted to make her stop but I knew she didn't like it when I touched her, so I washed the cream off my face and put toothpaste on my toothbrush and started with my teeth.

"Mom and Dad really let you have it during dinner tonight," I said, my mouth filled with toothpaste. I brushed around my braces, which is hard because you have to get in between the wires and the rubber bands and the little train track things, and sometimes the bristles break if you do it the wrong way.

Deborah didn't say anything. She watched me brush up and down, up and down.

"Mom seemed really mad," I offered.

"I hate how melodramatic she is," said Deborah. "Did you see all the paint on her hands? And in her hair? It was disgusting."

"She works hard," I said. "She was in her studio last night until midnight and then all day today too. She's trying to finish *Child in the Rain* in time for the opening."

"She's been trying to finish that stupid painting for years. And it still stinks."

I didn't say anything. I loved every inch of that painting.

"She's such a drama queen," said Deborah. "I can't believe she brought up all that stuff with Artie sitting right there. She was just dying to make me look stupid in front of him. And so were you. Reciting poetry and quoting from the dictionary like that. I hate this family."

I frowned and sat down on the closed toilet seat across from Deborah. Our knees touched. Deborah drew her legs closer to her body.

"I didn't mean to make things worse."

"Yes, you did," said Deborah. "You did it after school too, telling Artie about how I cried during *Charlotte's Web*. Why would you tell him that, Miriam? That was such a long time ago."

"I just wanted him to know that there's more to you than meets the eye."

There was a pause. We stared at each other for a moment. And then, without speaking, we both rose and looked into the mirror together the way we always used to, her black hair against my mousy brown, her face against my face. We hadn't done this in a long time. Our faces had always been different. Something about my nose and Deborah's cheeks and the way our mouths were shaped, but this time the differences were alarming. We didn't even look like we came from the same family.

"It's weird to think that a woman like our mother could have two daughters that turned out so different from each other," Deborah said.

"I know," I breathed, my voice catching.

"You know, you really should do something about yourself, Miriam. You should hear the things Jenny Clarke was saying about you when I was over there. Now, even the high school kids know about you. They were all laughing at you."

I imagined Deborah, surrounded by her friends, and I couldn't help wondering, was she laughing too?

Deborah stared into the mirror, her face still pressed against mine. Her cheeks were flushed, and her eyes looked tired. Then she drew her face away and started braiding her long black hair, her hands moving in careful, practiced rhythms. "They're my friends," she said, as if she read my mind. "I couldn't say anything."

"Mom always says that the masses are asses," I reminded her.

"Mom is wrong."

"She just wants us to make something of ourselves."

Deborah laughed. "You know what they want? They want to live in a fantasy world. They want us to be better than all the other kids in Carlton, so they don't have to feel so bad about moving here."

I backed away from my reflection and sat down on the edge of the bathtub. The porcelain was cold behind my knees. Something inside me clenched like a fist. I didn't want to hear any more. Something about Deborah's words made me want to cover my ears with both my hands and block out whatever truth might be in there. Instead, I sat there with my eyes open, looking at the way her body curved beneath the lavender bathrobe.

"Why haven't you told Mom and Dad about what's happening to you at school?" she said. I didn't answer, so she went on. "Miriam, whenever you walk past your locker you get teased. Right? I know that. It was the same way for me. How come you haven't walked into Mom's studio and told her how bad things are? How come you haven't gone into Dad's office while he's grading papers and had a good old heart-to-heart? Why don't they know how bad it is?"

"Because . . ." I stammered, feeling the lie coming, feeling myself aching to believe what I was about to say, "because they have enough on their minds. Dad's been trying so hard to get tenure.

And Mom's always staying up late getting ready for the opening. They have enough to worry about."

Deborah sat down across from me on the closed toilet seat. She pushed a strand of hair back behind my ear. I leaned my head into the palm of her hand for a moment and closed my eyes.

"That's not why you haven't told them," Deborah said. "You haven't told them for the same reason I didn't tell them. You know they wouldn't do a damn thing about it. They would congratulate you for marching to your own drum and tell you that the masses are asses, and then they would send you right back into school like some kind of hero."

"That's not true," I whispered.

"It is," said Deborah. "Mom and Dad are wrong. People don't respect you for your differences. They hate you."

"Artie doesn't hate me," I sniffled.

"He thinks you're a kid."

"He calls me Shakespeare. He looks at me like he knows me."

Deborah almost smiled. She pushed another greasy strand of hair back behind my ear.

"Look at yourself. You aren't Artie's type, Miriam. He's not interested in little girls."

"I'm not a little girl. I'm twelve."

"You're a baby. You've barely been born."

"He speaks to me in Spanish," I told her. "He thinks I'm a poet."

Deborah frowned. "He tolerates you. But take my word for it. The girls that Artie dates are nothing like you. They're mature. They know what they're doing with boys. Do yourself a favor and stay away from him. Stop flirting with him. Stop following him around. You'll just make things worse for yourself. Stay away from Artie, Miriam. Stay away from things you're too young to understand."

"I'm not as young as you think I am," I whispered.

Deborah raised herself up and headed for the door. Then she turned around one last time.

"You're young enough," she said.

8

The next morning I came down for breakfast in my filmy organza nightgown. The one with ruffles down the front and the ribbon straps that make my arms look like swans. I know how to walk like a runway model. Rosie taught me. You have to stick your hips way out and lean your body back and glare at everyone like you have *attitude*. I walked down the stairs with my hips in front and my body back and then I floated from the stairwell to the kitchen table. Hips, Shoulders, Arms, Neck. Elbow-Elbow, Wrist-Wrist-Wrist. My filmy organza nightgown trailed behind me.

Deborah was already sitting at the table with Artie. She had half a grapefruit and was taking tiny grasshopper bites as if taking human bites would make her fat. Artie was reading poetry out loud from a thin red book, and he gestured with his long fingers while he read. There is nothing more sexy than a man who reads poetry out loud at the breakfast table. I brought a bowl of Cheerios to the table and started to eat. I tried to make sure Artie could see my tongue when I brought the spoon to my lips. Sometimes I licked the rim of the spoon all the way around and breathed heavily so my breath fogged up the silver.

"What's wrong with you?" said Deborah.

"I like the texture of the spoon," I panted. "It feels good in my mouth."

"Jenny Clarke is right," she muttered. "You are a freak."

"No, I'm not. I'm sensitive. Things touch me that don't touch other people. Poets are like that, right, Artie? Don't you find that the more you read poetry the more heightened your senses become?"

"Well," Artie said, raising his cereal spoon and running his tongue across the rim to test my theory, "I don't know that my senses are heightened exactly, but poetry does get you to notice stuff. So if that's what's getting you to lick your spoon, I guess it's cool."

Artie and I both ran our tongues across our spoons while Deborah took another microscopic bite of grapefruit.

"What are you reading, Artie?" I asked.

"Pablo Neruda. He wrote love poems. He'd be into your spoon theory."

"Artie's been reading them to me," Deborah told me, putting one hand on Artie's shoulder like she owned him.

I put my hand on Artie's other shoulder. "I would love to hear you read, Arthur."

"Okay." Artie smiled at me. "It's pretty sexy stuff, though. Neruda was known for using a lot of erotic imagery. But it's translated from Spanish, so a lot gets lost in translation."

"I can take it," I said, moving the spoon in my mouth.

Artie looked a little embarrassed, but he started reading anyway. Deborah kept her hand on his shoulder and I leaned in with my spoon so that I could look at the words while he read. I made my lips move when his lips moved.

> *"Your breast is enough for my heart,*
> *and my wings for your freedom.*
> *What was sleeping above your soul will rise*
> *out of my mouth to heaven.*

> *"Para mi corazón basta tu pecho,*
> *para tu libertad bastan mis alas.*
> *Desde mi boca llegará hasta el cielo*
> *lo que estaba dormido sobre tu alma."*

"Cool," Deborah said, looking at Artie.

"Subtle," I said.

Artie put the book down.

I tried again. "I love his use of words. The nouns are especially impressive."

Deborah glared at me.

"And the way he used metaphor. You could really feel how his love was like a bird swooping and rising up out of his aching soul."

Artie tousled my hair. "You're really something, Shakespeare."

"Oh, she's something all right," Deborah muttered.

"Hey, Artie, after we all get dressed, why don't you and I go up on top of Deborah's roof? You can bring Neruda and I can bring e. e. cummings. He writes love poems too, but his are quieter.

That's why he doesn't use capital letters. His poems have a lot of windiness in them, so I think they would sound good from on top of the roof."

Artie grinned at me. "Maybe later, Shakespeare. Deborah and I have big plans this morning."

"That's right," said Deborah. "Today I'm going to do something different. Something I've wanted to do for a long time."

I plopped three huge scoops of brown sugar into my Cheerios. "Another change? Great, Deborah. I love it when you change." I stirred my Cheerios with one finger. "I don't know if you realize this, Artie, but Deborah has been changing a lot lately. She's like the flavor of the day. Deborah du jour. So, Deborah, what are you going to change this time? You've already changed the way you dress, the way you talk, the way you act, the way you smell. What's left?"

Deborah picked up her dishes and headed over to the sink. "You are really messed up," she said. "This is something I've been thinking about a long time. Everyone in this family has long hair. You have long hair, Mom has long hair. Dad hasn't cut his hair in months. And I'm just as bad. My hair is almost down to my waist." Deborah reached around and pulled her black hair back into a ponytail. Then she let it go. It fell back in long, dark waves.

"Today I'm going to take it all off. I want to see my shoulders. I want to see my neck. So say goodbye to the old Deborah. When you see me again you won't even know who I am."

There was a picture of Deborah in the dining room that I had always loved. She was six or seven years old and she was standing by the piano with her little quarter-sized violin. She was wearing white stockings and a white Alice in Wonderland dress and she was standing up straight and tall the way they teach you to stand in Suzuki violin school, with your shoulders back and your head tipped and your violin nice and straight. But what I loved most about the photograph was Deborah's hair. It was held back in barrettes and it hung straight down below her waist. There was such a contrast between the white dress and the black hair. She was so tiny and the violin was so tiny and her hair was so long that she looked almost like a fairy.

"I'm going with her for moral support," said Artie. "I know it's going to be a big step."

My Cheerios tasted stale. I took my spoon and crushed the rest of them down until every single loop was so soggy that it would never rise to the surface again.

"Cheer up, Shakespeare," said Artie. "Why don't you come along? We could bring Neruda with us. I could show you how to do some translations."

Deborah stared at me. Secretly, imperceptibly, she shook her head no. If I wasn't her sister, I wouldn't have noticed. It was a psychic message built on years of secret communication. If she shook her head and thought *no* hard enough, maybe I would change my mind.

I touched the cover of Neruda's book with one finger. "Sure, Artie, I'd love to come along," I said.

9

It didn't take us long to zip across town to Giorgio Gigante's Hair Salon. Giorgio has been our barber since we were little girls. He has a kind of shiny baldness that makes you want to rub his head and make a wish. He must polish his head in the mornings because it is always immaculately clean and pink. He has more than enough hair in other places, though, to make up for his lack of hair on top. A long dark mustache sticks out and curls at the corners, and thick, dark hair grows on the backs of his hands and down his open shirt. He probably has hair down his back too, but my mother tells me it wouldn't be polite to ask.

Giorgio wears real gold chains, and what he claims is a real two-million-dollar diamond stud in his ear. One time when I said it was pretty, Giorgio told me he had been given all his valuable jewelry as tokens of esteem for being the best barber in the world. The real two-million-dollar diamond, he said, was a gift from the king and queen of Istanbul. He said he flew all the way to Istanbul three times a year just to give them haircuts.

"He's a royal barber," I told Artie with a sly smile.

Artie and I sat together on the pink vinyl couch as Giorgio began to cut Deborah's hair. The first cut was the hardest to watch because Giorgio held his scissors close to her neck and combed down right past her ear. He cut straight across so the hair fell around her feet like strands of a horse's tail. I had Artie's copy of Neruda open on my lap, and every now and then one or the other of us would read a line. My Spanish was nowhere as good as Artie's, but I could pronounce it, and it was fun to make my voice sound poetic in a different language. I scooted over so my shoulder was leaning against Artie's bare arm. I peered down into the book.

> *"Oh la boca mordida, oh los besados miembros,*
> *oh los hambrientos, dientes, oh los cuerpos trenzados."*

When I looked up, I saw Deborah's hair falling to the floor like black feathers, but I tried to keep focused on Artie and on the love poems and on the shoulder that was pressing against me.

"If some guy said those words to me, I would give him anything he wanted," I said.

Artie laughed, but he was staring at Deborah as the barber took another lock of her hair between his fingers and cut right across. Now her white neck was exposed. You could see the arc of her shoulder.

"Don't most women in Spain have long hair?" I asked.

"Neruda is from Chile," Artie told me.

"But he appreciates femininity. Think of it. He's in love with some gorgeous girl with long hair like the waves of the sea, or something like that, and then suddenly she goes and cuts it all off.

Now what is he going to say, your hair is like blades of grass? Your hair is like the stubby fingers of wind across a chopped field? It just isn't the same."

Deborah's hair kept falling around her chair.

"Neruda appreciated anything sensual," Artie said. "Shoulders, for instance. And necks. Neruda loved necks." Artie's eyes were wide open now, and he started tapping nervously with one foot. I could feel the vibrations all through the pink vinyl seat. I could feel Artie breathing next to me.

"Neruda was wrong," I told him. "Sensuality isn't everything. Sometimes it's the quirky chicks who really have something to say. I knew we should have brought e. e. cummings. Who reads Chilean poets anymore, anyway?"

Artie nodded absently, but he never stopped watching Deborah's reflection in the mirror as more and more of her neck and shoulders were exposed. When Giorgio was done cutting he picked up a pink blow-dryer and started combing his fingers through what was left of her hair. Deborah lifted her chin and closed her eyes.

"*Oh la cópula loca de esperanza y esfuerzo,*" said Artie.

My stomach felt like lead.

Deborah gave Giorgio Gigante some money and walked up to us, smiling. She turned her head from side to side. The transformation was alarming and complete. Deborah was wearing the white sweater that Mom and Dad brought back from Italy last fall and the new short hair showed off the curve of her neck and shoulders. She looked so confident and mature and sexy. Nothing like the loser she had been when we both were in elementary school. Nothing like the sister who played the violin and liked to look at her reflection with me in the bathroom mirror. Nothing like our mother, whose hair was always rising from her head like smoke. It didn't matter that she couldn't understand poetry as well as I could. She was a goddess. She was the reason men wrote poetry in the first place.

Artie took her hand and bowed. "*Quiero hacer contigo lo que la primavera hace con los cerezos.* I want to do with you what the spring does with the cherry trees. That's Neruda too. God, you look delicious, Deborah."

"Thank you, Artie," Deborah whispered.

I could feel the two of them leaning toward each other.

"I think you looked better the other way," I told her.

"Be quiet, Miriam," Deborah said.

I bent down and picked up the book of poetry. For once I had nothing to say. I was quiet when Artie helped Deborah with her jacket. I was quiet when he held the door for her. I was quiet even when we got into the ancient yellow Volkswagen convertible. I kept my lips pressed together so tight I looked like a fish. I didn't say anything at all when Deborah slid into the front seat. I could have been born without a mouth. I could have been like Papageno in *The Magic Flute.* He's the one who told too many stories, and the fairies put a padlock on his lips so all he could say was "mmm-mmph." I pinched my mouth closed with my fingers so that my lips flattened out. I squeezed so hard it felt like I was putting a padlock on my mouth too.

I didn't say anything when Artie put the key in the ignition and started his car. Then he yawned and stretched and put his arm around the back of Deborah's seat, his brown hand massaging her shoulder, one long finger sliding gently up and down her neck. I stretched my feet out so the heels of my sneakers pushed into Deborah's seat. I pushed so hard, I thought they would rip through the vinyl.

Deborah didn't say anything either. She just turned on the radio and leaned her head over to the side so Artie could trace one brown finger back and forth across her shoulder.

"*Cuerpo de mujer mía, persistiré en tu gracia,*" he sighed.

10

On weekends, Artie would get himself all set up at the kitchen table with a can of soda and a bowl of yellow cheese doodles. He would put his feet on the table and read *Hamlet* to himself out loud. When I walked in today, Artie was practicing Act Three, Scene Two, which is my favorite because it's the play within a play. Hamlet is at the theater. He's acting all crazy around Ophelia, trying to get her to believe he's going insane. So, Act Three, Scene Two has an actor playing an actor watching a play during a play, and that's pretty darn complicated, if you ask me. Shakespeare must have been a genius. Otherwise, he never would have come up with something so puzzling. But I have always liked puzzles.

Artie was having a hard time being both Hamlet and Ophelia. He kept on changing his voice when he read Ophelia's lines, which was hilarious because he would make his Ophelia voice go all squeaky and soft. "Lady, shall I lie in your lap? *No, my lord.* I mean, my head upon your lap? *Ay, my lord.* Do you think I meant country matters? *I think nothing, my lord.*" Artie popped two yellow cheese doodles into his mouth and washed them down with soda. He scribbled something in the margin of his script with a pen. Then he practiced again. Hamlet and Ophelia, Hamlet and Ophelia, Hamlet and Ophelia.

I walked over to him and plunged my hand into the bowl of cheese doodles. I popped a few in my mouth and licked the yellow crumbs off my fingers. "Where's Deborah?" I asked him with my mouth full.

Artie looked up from his script and smiled. "I think she and Judy Clarke are up in her room cramming for the English midterm. She told me she hasn't even read half the books. Your mom is going to kill her if she brings home another C."

I sat in the chair next to him and put my bare feet up on the table so that our ankles were touching. "Studying your lines?"

Artie took a swig of soda and nodded.

"Do you want me to help you? I could be Ophelia. I've been listening to you practice that scene for so long I think I already have the lines memorized," I said. "I like Ophelia. She stays by Hamlet's side even though he's losing his marbles. I think even crazy people deserve to have friends, don't you? Except, I guess technically Hamlet isn't really crazy. He's just pretending to be crazy so it doesn't really count. Everyone knows the one who *really* has mental problems is Ophelia." Artie gave me a funny look but I went on talking. "I mean, come on. She jumps in the river and drowns herself at the end of the play. What could be worse than that?" I grabbed Artie's soda and chugged it really loud so you could hear each gulp going down. Then I wiped my mouth with the back of my hand.

Artie grinned at me. "You are such a strange kid," he said.

I crossed my eyes, stuck out my tongue, and punched him in the shoulder. Artie pinned my arm behind my back. Then he leaped off his chair and tickled me until I was spluttering with giggles and had snot and spit all over my face. It was wonderful.

"Okay," said Artie, "you can be Ophelia. You passed the test."

I picked myself off the floor and wiped my nose with the back of my hand. "Thanks."

Artie handed me a tissue and a copy of the script. He talked to me while I cleaned off my face. "So. Some background. Hamlet is being kind of a jerk here. He's flirting with Ophelia, but he's also kind of trying to confuse her. The thing you need to know is that Ophelia is really in love with him. So even though she's sort of scared of how weird he's acting, she wants him to stick around. Do you think you can handle that, Shakespeare?"

I grinned. "I can handle anything," I said.

"Okay, so here we go. *Lady, shall I lie in your lap?*"

I tapped my script and frowned.

"You are supposed to say, *No, my lord,*" said Artie.

"It says here you're supposed to lie down with your head on my lap. You're just standing there like a penguin. I can't be Ophelia if you're just standing there like a penguin. Come on, Artie. If you don't put your head in my lap, I have no reason to say my line." Artie didn't move. He looked uncomfortable. I pulled on his sleeve. "Come on. Be Hamlet. I can't help you rehearse unless you put your heart into this."

"Okay," said Artie, pointing at me with one big finger. "But don't get any ideas." Artie and I sat down on the kitchen floor and then Artie lowered himself down so that his head was on my lap and he was looking up at me with sparkling eyes. "*Lady, shall I lie in your lap?"* I could feel the weight of his head on the tops of my legs. I wanted to put my fingers in his hair so badly it hurt.

"No, my lord," I said.

Artie looked into my eyes. *"I mean, my head upon your lap?"*

Artie had the most amazing eyes I had ever seen. They were a kind of greenish brown, almost gold, and they had tiny flecks of gray around the rim. I gazed into his eyes. *"Ay, my lord."*

Artie reached up and touched the line from my jaw to my chin. *"Do you think I meant country matters?"* His fingers were smooth.

"I think nothing, my lord," I whispered.

Just then, Deborah and Judy tumbled down the stairs with their crib notes and their English binders. They saw Artie and me on the kitchen floor. They saw Artie with his head in my lap. They saw me looking down at him.

Artie and I both scrambled to our feet. And then all four of us looked at each other without saying anything. Without breathing.

"Hey, Fisher," Judy finally giggled, "you better keep your baby sister away from your boyfriend. She's so goddamn gorgeous. He might leave you for her." She nearly fell over, she was laughing so hard.

Deborah grinned and then she was laughing too. "If it was anyone else, I'd be worried," she said.

Artie looked at me and then he looked at Deborah and Judy. He put his arm around my shoulders and squeezed me so hard I thought I would die. "I'll tell you something," he sputtered, "she may not be much to look at, but she's one hell of an Ophelia." And then everyone laughed. Even me. I clenched the script in my fist and forced my lips to smile and I laughed and laughed and laughed.

11

Laughter
rises out of the stomach
like fire
spits from the pores
burns, sears, scours
singes off hair
rips razors across wrists
leaves notes without any answers

Miss Garland perched on top of her stool like some kind of color-ful bird. She was wearing a long Indian print skirt with tassels and mirrors and floral elephants holding each other's tails. She was try-ing to get us to talk about *Romeo and Juliet,* but it wasn't working. It was the last class before lunch. Kids leaned across desks. Kids rolled their eyes and chewed on pencils. Kids doodled disturb-ing things in their notebooks: people's heads with daggers stuck in the eye sockets, nuclear submarines, broken hearts with worms streaming out. Some kids had their feet up on their desks. Some kids were looking out the window or at the clock or at their fingernails. The watermelon girls sat in the corner all together and wrote notes on each other's notebooks. Every once in a while, one of them would whisper something and they would all break out laughing. Jenny Clarke sat behind me. She kept tapping the side of her desk with her pencil. *Tap tap. Tap tap tap.*

"Quit it," I whispered, without turning around.

Tap tap. Tap tap tap.

"Quit it!" I growled.

Tap tap tap tap.

Miss Garland moved down the aisles of the classroom and read Shakespeare to us. Her torn copy of *Romeo and Juliet* cut back and forth across the space between our desks. "Now, pay attention," she told us. "They see each other. They can tell right away they have an attraction for each other. Romeo starts flattering her, telling her how beautiful she is. But Juliet's not sure. Things seem to be moving too fast. Can anyone in here relate to that? Come on, guys. Wake up. Jenny Clarke, what do you think? Does this sound familiar?"

Some boy in the back row made a meowing sound. Misty Marin and Tracy Blair giggled. Jenny turned around and glared at them. "Actually, I *do* know someone who can relate to Juliet," Jenny said. "But I'm not sure I should talk about it. It's personal."

Miss Garland stopped in her tracks and smiled at all of us. "Don't worry about getting personal," she said. "It's good to speak from your heart. How else are we going to understand Shakespeare? We have to find ourselves in his words. Go on please."

"Well. It's this *friend* of mine." Jenny made her fingers squish like two quotation marks around the word *friend*.

"Ooh, who's your *friend*, Jenny?" hooted the boy in the back row.

Miss Garland waved at the boy. "Ignore him," she said. "And remember, class, anything that Jenny tells us stays in this room. Does everyone understand me?"

The watermelon girls nodded their heads.

Jenny put her shoulders back. "Okay," she said. "I'll tell you something personal. But you have to promise not to laugh."

You could feel the different kids in the room—the nail-biters, the out-the-window-lookers, the note-writers, the desk-leaners, the popular kids, the unpopular kids—all staring at Jenny, who was about to reveal something about herself. Maybe she was going to tell us about things we had heard but never knew for certain. Maybe she was going to tell us why her mother was with a different boyfriend every weekend. Maybe she was going to tell us why she never did her homework, or why she never brought a lunch. Maybe she was going to tell us why they held her back last year. Maybe she was going to tell us why she spent so many afternoons in Principal Russo's office, staring at the wall.

"Tell us anything you want," Miss Garland said. "The door is open."

Jenny swiveled around in her chair. She talked right to the watermelon girls. As if they were the only ones in the room who existed. "Okay. Here's the story. I have this friend who is totally into this boy. She thinks he's her soul mate and everything, just like Juliet. But there are problems. See, this guy she's in love with, he wouldn't even think of kissing her because, frankly, my friend looks exactly like a boy. No hips. No boobs. Nothing."

The watermelon girls grinned.

"That sounds difficult," said Miss Garland.

"It is. Especially since . . . Can I speak openly here?"

"Of course," Miss Garland said, putting her hand on Jenny's shoulder. "Jenny can speak openly without having to worry about negativity, right, everyone?"

Everyone nodded.

"Well, you see, this friend of mine, she's never kissed a boy. But she really wants to. Are you sure it's okay for me to talk about this?"

"Of course," Miss Garland coaxed. "It relates directly to the play. Juliet had never been with a boy either, remember? And then she meets Romeo and that all changes. Don't censor yourself, Jenny. Tell us. What's keeping your friend from getting what she wants?"

"She's a *freak*," Jenny said.

I held myself still.

"She's such a freak the guy would rather puke than kiss her."

What was she saying? Was she talking about me?

"This weekend he was at my house," Jenny said. "He told me he would never kiss anyone as ugly and as pathetic as her."

The room was spinning. I couldn't catch my breath. That couldn't be true. All those things Jenny was saying about me. They couldn't be true. Artie wouldn't have confided in Jenny. He didn't even know Jenny. Tears started streaming down my face. Everyone leaning in could see it. No matter how I held my book, no matter how I lowered my eyes, they could see, because now my shoulders were shaking and the stupid, stupid sobs were coming out from somewhere inside my stomach and I was clutching the edge of my desk so hard my fingers hurt.

"That's enough," Miss Garland said to Jenny.

"I'm just talking about Shakespeare," Jenny said. "You told me to be honest."

"I said, that's enough. Now pick up your books and get out."

Jenny put a stick of gum in her mouth. She walked down the rows of seats to the back of the room where Misty Marin and Tracy Blair sat grinning. They both reached out to squeeze her hand as she walked by. Jenny blew a perfect round bubble. Then she slammed the door.

Miss Garland put her hand on my shoulder. "Why don't you go to the bathroom and clean yourself up," she whispered.

"Can I go with her?" It was Rosie, her voice rising up out of the fog.

"Of course. Of course, go with her."

And then Rosie was at my elbow helping to guide me out of the classroom, and I was crying harder than I've ever cried before, and the worst part was that I couldn't stop the sounds coming out of me—like I was some kind of animal, mooing and mooing and stumbling down the linoleum corridor to the girls' bathroom that would only be empty for fifteen more minutes until the lunch bell would ring.

12

The girls' bathroom smells like a combination of watermelon hand cream and antiseptic cleanser. Sometimes when you go about your life and a smell assaults you, it's just a moment of discomfort, a wrinkle of the nose, a breath of something offensive, and then it's over. But this smell is different. This smell goes straight to the back of your throat and strangles you with its sweetness. You could walk home at the end of the day, or climb into bed in the evening, and the smell would still be there, curling around your hair, curling into your skin. You could take a breath, and instead of getting air you would get this: a reminder that seventh grade will never go away.

I stumbled into the bathroom and dropped to the cold, hard tile. I hugged my knees, rocking out my fury, sobs rushing out of me like they had been building since the day that Artie arrived, from before that, from the day that Deborah started looking at me like I *was* a freak, from the day I walked into the middle school hallway and the first group of girls turned their faces away. All my frustration poured out. I cried until there wasn't anything left. Rosie draped herself around me, her red bird's-nest hair springing out everywhere, against my cheek and nose and shaking shoulders. She kept on saying, "Forget her, baby. You just put her out of your mind. You're better than that. Come on, baby girl. Stop crying. Stop crying." She got up and unrolled a roll of toilet paper. "Blow," she said.

"All those things Jenny said about Artie."

"Listen to me, Miriam. She was just trying to get at you. Jenny Clarke has real problems."

"She's a slut. That's her problem."

"That's not nice," Rosie said with a little smile.

"But it's true." I stood up and looked at my face in the mirror. "You know it is. I'm going to be a famous writer when I grow up. What do you think will happen to Jenny Clarke? I'm psychic. I can see her now—leaning against the old factory on the corner of Main and Fillmore. What's she doing? Oh my God! She's wearing a feather boa and fishnet stockings. No one is surprised. They drive by in their cars. They shake their heads and throw a few quarters at her and they say, Yeah, we always knew she was a slut."

"Stop it, Miriam," whispered Rosie.

"Why? It's true. Everyone knows she's worthless. Even the teachers know it."

"Miriam. Trust me. Stop it."

Which is when I took a breath. Which is when I looked and saw Rosie's face, white and worried and shaking silently *no*, which is when I heard the slightest rustle behind me like a body shifting its weight from one hip to another, which is when I turned around in slow motion, slower than I had ever turned around before, because

I knew, without knowing how I knew, that Jenny Clarke was in the doorway and that she had heard all those things I had said, and that something very bad was going to happen.

"So, you think I'm a slut?" Jenny said.

"Miriam didn't mean it," Rosie said. "She was just blowing off steam."

Jenny Clarke took a step forward and I took a step back.

"Take it easy, Jenny," Rosie begged. "Miriam's just mad because of what you said in English class. We know you're not a slut, okay? She was just kidding."

"I want to hear it from the Freak," Jenny said.

"Tell her," Rosie said to me.

"Tell her what?"

"Tell her you didn't mean what you said."

Jenny Clarke took another step forward. I didn't move. I couldn't. Something in me had iced over and I wanted to stay and fight.

"I'm not sorry," I whispered. "I meant what I said."

"You're gonna get it, Miriam Fisher," Jenny hissed. "You don't even know what I could do to you. You don't even know how miserable you could be. I have a lot of friends."

"You don't scare me," I said.

Jenny pushed me hard into the white bathroom sink. "You should be scared," she breathed. "You should be scared, you ugly little Freak."

Jenny stormed out of the bathroom. The door closed behind her. I threw myself into the nearest stall and knelt on the floor. It all came up. All my words. My stomach. All of it. I gripped the edge of the toilet bowl with cold, shaking hands and heaved my misery into the water.

13

GIRL

They knew who she was.
When they looked at her,
they could see what would happen.
She would end up alone:
leaning against some street corner,
crumbling brick, iron bars,
smokestacks, and they would think—
I knew this about her.
Even before it happened
I could see it coming, like a storm
in the distance, dark and cold as rain.

You can see the whole neighborhood from the top of Deborah's
roof: the row of factory houses, the old mill, and, farther down,
where the road bends into brush, the rusted-out railroad tracks. If
you strain your eyes, you can see the middle school on the other

side of town with its metal flagpole and its concrete blocks. Up on my sister's roof, it was the kind of October day that makes you want to cry, the leaves scratching across the concrete whenever the wind blew. You could see them coming down from the bare branches of oaks that lined the walk. If I kept my eyes on the leaves, I could almost forget what had happened between me and Jenny.

"What are you writing about?" Artie said, leaning over my shoulder.

I closed Clyde's cover and turned away. "Nothing." I exhaled. "I like coming out here to read my work out loud."

Artie smiled. "Neruda used to compose that way too. Maybe you and Neruda would have been pals if he was twelve and if you lived in Chile." I shivered and Artie moved closer to me. I could feel his shoulder next to my shoulder. "I can see why you like coming up here to write. You can see everything from up here."

We both looked out at the neighborhood in silence for a while. Then Artie took a deep breath and let it out.

"Miriam. Listen. About the other day."

"I don't want to talk about that," I said.

"Well, just listen then. You were a great Ophelia. You're such a natural. You could be a real actress if you wanted. You even had me believing you. I'm sorry I laughed when Deborah and Judy came down. But it was so awkward, you know? I just didn't know how else to react."

I hugged my arms around myself.

Artie paused for a moment. Then he said, "Miriam, have any kids at the middle school said anything about you and me?"

I caught my breath. I could hear Jenny Clarke's voice, the bile of her words. I wanted to disappear. I wanted to rewind my life and be nine years old again.

"Because the night after Deborah and Judy saw us rehearsing, we were at this party, and Judy was really teasing me. I might have said some things I didn't mean."

"No one said anything to me," I whispered.

But I could hear Jenny's voice again, repeating the words she said came from Artie, *The sight of her makes him sick, the sight of her makes him sick.* And then I imagined Artie, with a beer in his hand, telling all the kids how disgusting I was, telling them how repulsive and ugly and pathetic I was. Telling them he would rather vomit than kiss me. So it was true. It was true. It was true.

"I don't know what happens," Artie said, "but when kids get together they get so mean. And they push you around a little. And maybe you laugh and join in just to get them off your back, you know? And you don't even think about what could happen. You're in the middle of a bunch of kids who are goofing off and saying stuff. And without thinking, you're laughing with them. And before you know it, you could be saying any old thing. Just words. And maybe you regret it later but there it is. You've said something stupid and there's nothing you can do."

Artie took a breath.

The wind blew the leaves in circles on the pavement.

"Hey, you're my buddy, right, Shakespeare? You're my best pal."

"Sure," I whispered.

The wind blew. All around us, leaves fell from the trees and skimmed across the concrete. We could hear a dog barking in the distance.

Artie moved closer to me. He leaned his shoulder against my shoulder.

Then Deborah appeared.

At the sight of her, Artie straightened up and turned, watching as my sister climbed out of her window and balanced her way across the flat roof to where we were sitting.

"Hey," said Deborah. "Judy Clarke's having another party tomorrow night. Her mother's gone for the weekend again. We'll go together like we did last time, right? Everyone will be there."

Artie looked at me.

"What's going on?" asked Deborah.

"Nothing," Artie said, looking down.

"Artie, you were so funny at Judy's. Everyone's still talking about how funny you were."

I stared at him.

"Artie," Deborah said, moving his face back to her. Deborah took both of Artie's hands. They must have been cold from the wind because she rubbed them together and then brought them to either side of her face.

Deborah moved closer and closer to Artie until their lips touched. And then it was more than lips. I sat on the roof and watched their mouths moving in slow circles. Leaves swirled down from the trees and all around the wind blew. Deborah and Artie held each other and kissed. I hugged my knees close to my chest and tried to imagine how it would feel to disappear.

14

The cafeteria. Old pizza burgers, taco sauce, tuna fish sandwiches, Tater Tots. If you are part of a group, it's easy. You know where to sit because your group has a designated table.

The exchange students sit close to the stage. They have strange haircuts, and they speak in strange accents, and everyone stays away from them. The *Dungeons and Dragons* geeks sit by the windows with their eight-sided dice and their maps and their little figurines. The popular kids sit at the back table. The boys on the football team wear strong deodorant and team jerseys and expensive sneakers. The popular girls drape themselves on the boys like sweaters. They have beautiful hair. They eat salads and laugh in loud voices. Standing together with their backs against the windows are the lunch monitors. If something like a hot dog bun or an empty pudding container goes flying across the room, they turn their faces away.

I usually sit with Rosie in the corner by the windows, but on Tuesdays and Thursdays Rosie has band, and on those days I have to fend for myself. I walked up and down the aisles looking for a place to sit. Sometimes there was an empty seat, but the girl sitting next to it would glare at me, or move her backpack so I couldn't get in. Sometimes I heard someone whisper "Freak," and then another person at that table would giggle. I kept walking, trying not to make eye contact with anybody.

Mary Barnes was sitting alone at a table near the back corner. She was eating a bag of potato chips and reading the scenes from *Romeo and Juliet* that were due that day in English. She had a copy of *CliffsNotes* next to her and she kept switching from the play to the notes to the play to the notes. She reached into the bag of potato chips and put two or three in her mouth. Then she wiped her chin and took a sip of chocolate milk. I brought my tray to her table and stood across from her. I took a breath.

"Do you mind if I sit here?"

She shrugged.

I sat down in the round orange seat, unwrapped my pizza burger, and took a bite. The bread was stale and the burger tasted like cardboard. I wished I had brought Clyde with me. If I had brought Clyde I could have written a sonnet to stale pizza burgers. *Thy rancid smell assaults my woeful nose.* But I didn't have Clyde, so I had to write my poem on a napkin in ketchup, which I guess is better than nothing. It's hard to write in ketchup. Ketchup gets smudged on your fingers, so whenever you try to make a letter it comes out looking like a thumbprint. That's probably why no one ever tried to market ketchup packets as writing utensils.

Then, *Ping.*

I felt something hit me in the back. A rolled-up piece of paper.

I turned around, unrolled the piece of paper, and looked at it. It said MIRIAM FISHER + ARTIE ROSENBERG. There were two stick figures. The one that was supposed to be me had round glasses and stringy hair and huge, erupting, volcanic pimples. She was standing with her arms and legs wrapped around the one that was supposed to be Artie. Her mouth was puckered and waiting. The one that was supposed to be Artie was throwing up all over her. There were pencil lines leading from his mouth into her mouth.

I crumpled the paper back into a ball, squeezing my hand into a fist. The corners of the paper pressed into my skin. I dropped my head down onto the table and tried to block it out but it kept on coming, all the noise, the roaring noise of all the other kids, like a wave growing larger.

I could hear the muffled sounds of people trying not to laugh. I could hear giggles and the *shhhhhh* of someone trying to quiet them down, and the eruption of laughter again. I should have kept my head on the table. The cool, smooth surface was a comfort. But I had to be stupid and turn my face into the crook of my arm so that I could see the table behind me. The watermelon girls were staring at me and smiling. There was Misty Marin at the center of the table with her perfect hair and her perfect lips and her perfect arms crossed in front of her perfect bosoms, and there was Tracy Blair sitting right next to her. Jenny Clarke was there too, perched as close as she could get to them, her skinny legs crossed at the knees.

I picked up my tray and walked as fast as I could without running.

Ping.

A Tater Tot sailed over the cafeteria and hit me between the shoulder blades. *Ping.* Another one. *Ping.* Another one. *Ping.* Another one. I held my tray with both hands and kept on walking without looking back.

15

The door to my mother's studio was half-open. I could see her sitting on the wooden stool with her back to me, gazing at the canvas but not painting. There were half-finished paintings all over the place: self-portraits, her own lined face screaming in rage, twisted in fury; paintings of Brooklyn, of old Jewish women pushing shopping carts down the cracked streets, heads covered in kerchiefs; paintings of nudes, not beautiful bodies, but bodies of older women, mothers with sinking breasts and cesarean scars, grandmothers with bent spines and white bellies hanging like used pillows, emaciated women crouched in shadows.

My mother sat on her stool with all of this around her. She sat and stared at the canvas. She had a thin brush in her hand. She sat and sat and didn't paint.

I knocked on the open door.

"Not right now, Miriam," my mother said, her back still to me.

"I was wondering if you had a second," I said.

My mother turned around on her stool and saw me standing in

the doorway. She rose from her seat. I came in, walking slowly. I always walk slowly in my mother's studio because there are so many things in there that make me want to stop and look. She was working on *Child in the Rain*. It was the first time I had seen it up close in almost a year. There was the little girl crouched on the front steps of a concrete building, steel bars on the windows, the background of a city street stretching off in the distance. The girl was holding her knees. Her back was curved and her long hair fell around her face because it was raining. You could see the puddles in front of the steps and how the rain glazed the cracks in the street. I always wondered why she was sitting on the steps, why she didn't just turn around and go into the building. But she crouched there on the steps with the rain coming down and the city darkening around her.

"It looks good," I told her.

"It's getting there," my mother said. "I have a long way to go."

"Do you think it'll be ready in time for the opening?"

My mother stood back and looked at it. "I hope so," she said.

I stood next to her and we looked at the painting together in silence. I wanted so badly to tell her what had been happening at school, I thought I would break open right there.

The girl in the painting was hugging her knees and you could see her shoulder blades. The way the girl's back curved under her shirt, and the way her hair fell in front of her face, made me think maybe I could talk to my mom because maybe she already knew what I was feeling. Maybe she was just waiting for me to say the words out loud so she could take me into her arms like she used to when I was a little girl and rock me and say *I know, I know, shhh, shhhhh.*

When I was a little girl I used to stay home with my mother and watch her paint. I used to snuggle against her, and she would put her hand around my shoulders and I would bury my face in her hair and breathe the strong smell of her: the smell of paint and turpentine and cigarettes and whatever coffee she was drinking that day, and I would let the smell assault me and just breathe until I disappeared. I wanted to do that now. I wanted her arms around me so I could bury myself in her side and tell her the whole thing, but my mother was staring at the painting, not at me.

"It looks flat," she said. "Don't you think it looks flat? It needs more dimension."

"I don't think it looks flat. It just looks like it's been raining. Rain washes things out."

My mother took her paintbrush and touched another strand of hair across the girl's face. Then she took the gray and touched her brush under the girl's eyes. She made the gray smudge down and smoothed it with the side of her thumb. All of a sudden it looked like the girl was crying. It looked like she had been crying for days and that pretty soon there would be nothing left and the girl would be an empty can, crushed and thrown away. My mother took the gray and dragged it along the girl's cheeks and down her chin.

"It's amazing," I whispered. "She looks exactly like me."

My mother took a cigarette out of its pack and lit up. She inhaled, closed her eyes, and blew smoke out of her mouth. "It isn't you, sweetheart," she said, taking a step back to look at what she had done. "It's me. It's me as a little girl. Didn't you know that? That's the street where I grew up. That's Flatbush Avenue. And there, see that dark window? That was my room. That little girl is me. They're all self-portraits, didn't you know that?"

I stared at *Child in the Rain.* Then I stared at all of the other paintings of women, the nudes with their curved spines and their tired bodies. The faces of women screaming in fury, or tearing at their hair.

My mother dipped her brush in white and put a tiny fleck in the corner of the girl's eye. "Now, what did you want to say to me?"

I stared at the painting and I couldn't tell her anything.

"Nothing," I whispered. "I just wanted to see how things were going."

My mother reached out and brushed a strand of hair behind my ear. Then she went back to her painting. I moved away from her, and from the canvas, and from all the things I didn't want to talk about.

"Honey, shut the door on your way out," my mother called behind me.

16

Dear Clyde,

The Oxford English Dictionary *says this about the word* maze: *"To bring into a state of delirium. To stupefy. To craze. To put out of one's wits. To bewilder, perplex, or confuse."*

Something bad is happening in my head. Like a trapdoor opening. Like a never-ending series of hallways that lead one into another into another. I used to think life was like the mazes you get in coloring books. All you have to do is find the right way. But lately I've been thinking I was wrong. Maybe for some people there isn't a way out. Maybe some people get trapped, and no matter how hard they try, they're just going to spend their lives bumping into walls—stuck in the maze forever.

—M

That night I sat on the edge of the bathtub and watched Deborah get ready for bed. She put her hair back with a cloth headband.

Then she rubbed apricot scrub into her skin and rinsed it off with three splashes of warm water, *splash splash splash*. I watched the water drip from her cheeks down the line of her chin and into the white sink basin. She brushed her teeth, tops and bottoms, fronts and backs, and when she spit, the toothpaste came out in a tidy stream. *Spritz*. I watched the shape her mouth made while it pursed to spit. I tried to memorize it. Every inch of her, all of the habits that seemed so familiar. I wanted so badly to tell her what was happening inside me, but I didn't have the words.

"Deborah," I finally said.

She took a sip of water from the blue bathroom glass. She moved it around in her mouth and then spit it out. "What is it?"

"What did kissing Artie feel like?"

She took off the cloth headband and pulled one hand through her short black hair. She looked at me like she was trying to decide whether or not to answer my question and I could see her face flicker—but then she lowered herself onto the closed toilet seat and leaned forward like she wanted to confide in me, and suddenly there she was, my same old sister, telling me secrets like she always used to do. Our bare knees touched. I found myself desperate to listen even though listening hurt.

"It felt amazing," Deborah whispered.

"That's not very descriptive."

Deborah smiled. Her face was glowing. "It was the best kiss I've ever had," she said, her voice so quiet there was barely breath behind her words. "It drove me crazy. Just thinking about it makes me want to . . . I shouldn't be telling you this."

"Yes, you should," I said.

Deborah swallowed and then pulled the bathroom door shut.

"The thing is, I could tell he wanted to go further. I could tell that if you hadn't been there staring at us we would have gone back into my bedroom and he would have tried to go all the way."

"You would have let him?" I choked on my own words.

Deborah smoothed her nightgown over her bare knees. "I don't think I should be talking to you about this," she whispered.

"No. You have to tell me. Would you have let him?"

Deborah stood up and turned toward the mirror.

"Would you have gone all the way?"

She took a bottle of our mother's perfume out of the medicine cabinet. She lifted the glass stopper, placed one fingertip across the opening, and tilted the vial. Then she touched her finger to different spots on her body. The hollow of her neck. The bottom of her ear. And then farther down where her bathrobe opened. When she placed the perfume bottle back into the medicine cabinet, I could see that her hand was shaking.

17

Everyone was asleep. I could hear them in their rooms, the sounds of their shallow breathing cutting into the night. I could hear the sounds our house makes when things are quiet. The heat whistled through the vents in the floor. Downstairs, below the floorboards, I could hear the moaning of the refrigerator and the slow *ker-drip ker-drop* from the sink in the kitchen where Mom had left two big pots soaking from spaghetti and meatballs. Things were quieter in the second-floor bathroom. But the fluorescent lights around the mirror made a sound that you could hear only if you listened really close, like a mosquito far off, a thin, insistent whine.

I took Deborah's pink travel case out of my backpack and put it out on the bathroom sink. It smelled good. Like perfume and lilac powder. I unzipped the top and slid out the instruments I needed. They were shiny and smooth under the bathroom lights. Tweezer. Eyelash curler. Scissors. Razor. I felt almost like other girls, laying out all my instruments and looking at my face in the mirror. I turned my head from one side to the other, one profile and the next. Maybe this was how my mother looked at the faces of her self-portraits before she changed them. *This one isn't right. This needs to be fixed.*

First I rubbed my father's shaving cream on my legs and moved the razor from my ankle to my knee. All the hair came off. I could feel the cleared spot with my fingers, smooth skin, very feminine. I did it again and again and again. Ankle to knee and ankle to knee and ankle to knee, all the hair coming away and leaving girl-legs in their place. My legs weren't all that ugly with the hair gone. They were still skinny, and the knees still bulged out on the top like doorknobs, but they shone now and they felt like satin. It was a beginning.

I picked up the tweezer and turned on the bubble lights around the bathroom mirror. My eyebrows were nothing like other girls' eyebrows. The other girls in my class had eyebrows that arced like little wavelets over their eyes. My eyebrows were different. They weren't bushy, exactly, not like the squirrel tails that my father's eyebrows resembled, all gray and hairy—my eyebrows were more like caterpillars with a little extra in between. I don't know what happened to eyebrows in Carlton Middle School. At the end of sixth grade, everyone still had the eyebrows that God meant for them to have—woolly, shaggy, thick, thin, whatever. Then kids came back from summer vacation and on the first day of seventh grade every girl had movie-star eyebrows, all graceful and perfect. It was time to get with the program. I tried tweezing out each tiny hair, but pulling out my eyebrow hairs one by one was going to take forever, so I picked up the razor and started shaving. At first I shaved just a little bit, just the very tops and on the bridge of my nose, but then it looked so good, I kept on going with the razor, shaping and shaping and sculpting and sculpting and watching the little brown fuzz fall to the bathroom floor like caterpillar fur.

Without my leg hair or my eyebrow hair, I felt different. Like I was changing into something new. I was smoother, sexier, more mature. I looked at my face in the mirror. Now it was time for the biggest change of all. Giorgio Gigante always cut our hair with a fine-toothed black comb, but I didn't have a comb so I licked my hand and smoothed my hair out with my fingers. I used my fingernail to draw a part down the middle of my scalp. It didn't come out quite right. It started out straight, and then it sort of zigzagged in the back. But that was the best I could do. I didn't mind though. It wouldn't matter if I had no part at all. Deborah's hair was so full that you could barely see her scalp.

I took a handful of hair and started cutting. I liked the sound the scissors made. *Snip*. And a clump of hair fell to the ground at my feet. *Snip, snip.* And another, and another, until the floor around me was covered. It was amazing that all of it had come off of me. There was so much of it. *Snip*. One time Artie told me our hair is just like our fingernails. It's dead matter. It's not even made of the same kind of cells as our skin, and that's why it doesn't bleed when we cut it off.

I took my bangs in one fist and cut an inch off the bottom, but when I let go, I could tell it was uneven. The hair across my forehead was long on the sides and short in the middle. The only thing I could do was start at the shortest point and try to make it as straight as I could. I snipped straight across my bangs, over and over again, until all I had was about an inch of fuzz growing across my forehead. It looked like a misplaced eyebrow. I hated it. I took some hair from the side that was still long and combed it over the front. I cut it into bangs. But it fell back into place, and now I had two different lengths on the side of my head, so I cut the first side until it was even, and then I cut the other side so it was even with the first, and then I cut the back so it was even with both sides, and then I cut all three sides short so that there was more volume because everyone knows that girls need volume in their hair. Then it was over. There wasn't anything left to cut. I was finished. Ladies and gentlemen, I give you the new Miriam Fisher.

I stared at my new face in the mirror. My heart was pounding. All of the sounds of the old house—the lights, the heating vents, the breathing—seemed to get louder and higher until they swirled around my head. I thought I was going to pass out. What had I done? I didn't look like a woman. I didn't even look like a girl. There were bare patches in some spots and in other spots my hair stuck straight out. I had no eyebrows at all. I looked more like a reptile than a human. I stared at my reflection in the mirror and watched the naked eyes grow wide and terrified, the thin mouth turn down. The strange, new face looked back: cut, massacred, and amazed.

Dear Clyde,

I am not a human being. I am a lizard. I am under the blankets and I can't stop touching the bald patches I left on my scalp. It feels strange and scary to put my fingers up to my head and feel the smooth of my skin. Lizard cold. Lizard smooth. I thought my life couldn't be worse, but here it is, three o'clock in the morning, and it's worse. It's worse.

I can hear Artie and Deborah in the room next door. First I thought she was just talking in her sleep, but this is different. I can hear them moving in her bed behind the wall. I can hear the springs creak, and I can hear the sounds of their voices.

Deborah's pillow is four inches away on the other side of the wall. It could be my body it could be my face it could be my breathing. I lie here and I try to make myself listen but now I don't hear anything at all so I hold my breath and try to will my heart to stop beating.

—M

18

The next morning, I wore a sweatshirt with the hood pulled down over my face. No one talked to anyone at the breakfast table. Artie and Deborah came down at different times to make it look like nothing had happened, Artie with his backpack filled with books, Deborah with her shirt buttoned up, and both of them looking flushed and nervous. They didn't sit next to each other. They poured milk in their bowls and orange juice in their glasses. They opened their science textbooks and pretended to study. Sometimes they would tap their pencils or make their eyes look off into space as if they were trying to memorize something important. But I knew what they were really thinking about: the whispering and the breathing and the bedsprings. Deborah took tiny bites of her toast and kept wiping her lips with the napkin even though there weren't any crumbs. Every few seconds one of them would swallow and you could hear it because the room was quiet except for the clinking of spoons and the clock tick tick ticking. I pulled my hood over my eyes and counted the seconds. Almost almost almost time for school. One more minute. Almost. Almost. Tick tick tick.

My father shuffled his seminar notes and took a cup of coffee. "You're all so quiet this morning," he said. "It's like a funeral marched through here. Must be an exam day. Is that it? You kids have tests today?"

Artie gestured to his science textbook and nodded without looking up.

My mother came down the stairs in her bathrobe.

"Welcome to the land of the living," intoned my father.

My mother bowed. She made her way to the breakfast table and poured herself a cup of coffee. "I don't know why they concentrate so much on the sciences," she said. "If I was going to design a school, the kids would be creating things and performing music. Mother Earth. There's your science."

My father rubbed my mother's shoulder. "That's a nice fantasy. But Carlton Public has never been interested in progressive education. Standardize them till they drop. Right, Artie? It's got to be status quo. Turn them all into little clones of the system."

"Right," Artie said.

"Speaking of status quo," said Deborah, "I'm going to Judy's house tonight. We're going to study for a history test."

"On a Friday night?"

Deborah shrugged. "I've decided that school is important to me, Mother. If I don't study I'll be stuck in Carlton my whole life."

I put my head down on the table.

"Miriam, you don't look so good," my mother said. "Do you have a fever? Take off the hood. Let me feel your forehead." My mother reached over and, before I could move, pulled my hood back.

I turned my hairless lizard's face toward her. No eyebrows. No bangs.

My mother put down her coffee.

I could feel all of their eyes on me. Deborah's, Artie's, my father's, all of them speechless, holding their breath, waiting for me to explain what I had done to myself.

"I cut my hair," I whispered.

My mother reached out and touched my head. She ran one cool finger up and down the bald patches. She traced the line where my eyebrows had been. I had never felt my mother's fingers on that part of my face before. She stared at my head. No eyebrows. No bangs. All uneven and cut.

"Oh, honey," my mother breathed, "what on earth have you done to yourself?"

I got up from the table. "Nothing," I said. "I'm fine."

As if on cue, Artie and Deborah rose behind me, carrying their bowls and spoons to the sink. We gathered our backpacks, our jackets, our lunches in silence, and filed out to Artie's yellow Volkswagen convertible. Deborah and Artie sat in front. I slid into the back next to Artie's sweatshirt, a sandy beach blanket, and a six-pack of cola. No one said anything when Artie put the key in the ignition and the engine turned over like a slow protest. No one said anything to anybody all the way to the high school. Every once in a while Deborah would turn around and look at me, shaking her head in astonishment.

I watched the world pass by outside my window. The train station. The brick buildings. The boarded-up houses. We stopped at the red light on the corner of Jenny's street. There was the falling-down house. There was Jenny locking the door with a key.

The light turned green. Once again, the world passed by in silence.

When we pulled up in front of the high school, Deborah and Artie looked at each other for a long time.

"You go ahead," Artie said. "I'm going to drive Miriam."

Deborah got out of the car. Then she turned around and looked at me. She reached into the backseat and touched my arm. "Be careful today, Miriam." Then she shut the door.

I stayed in the backseat while Artie drove back down the road to Carlton Middle School. Every once in a while, he would make a noise like he wanted to say something to me, but he never did. He rounded the corner from Main Street onto School Street, and from School Street to the parking lot of Carlton Middle School, where kids rushed out of school buses and out of their parents' pickup trucks into the courtyard, backpacks bouncing on their backs like overstuffed balloons. I watched Artie watching the kids get off the rusted yellow buses and make their way into the building. We sat like that for a few minutes, me in the backseat, Artie in the front, neither of us saying anything to each other.

"I'm worried about you," Artie whispered finally. "Are you okay?"

The morning bell rang. Kids started rushing into the building. The flag whipped and blew on the flagpole. I pulled the hood tight over my head, slammed the car door, and made my way up the concrete steps to the school.

19

The hallways of Carlton Middle School are a war zone for someone like me. It's best if you get from one class to another as fast as possible—that way you minimize the risk. I can get from Mr. Humphrey's math class to Mr. Howard's social studies class in less than fifty seconds if I walk close to the lockers and carry all my books close to my body. I can get from Mr. Howard's social studies class to Mrs. Ferger's science class in two and a half minutes if I take the stairs behind the computer lab and then cut through the library, which is good because the kids who hate me usually stay out of there anyway. The switch that really gets me is the one from Mrs. Ferger's science class to Miss Garland's English class. There is no good way to get there. No matter how I do it, I have to pass right by the seventh-grade lockers and the girls' bathroom.

I tugged my hood tighter over my head so no one could see what I had done. Still, I felt my mistake underneath the cloth like a terrible secret waiting to be exposed. I hugged my science book, my French workbook, and my copy of *Romeo and Juliet*. And then there was my math folder, my calculator, my English binder, and Clyde. On top was my pencil case and my paper-bag lunch. You're not allowed to take your backpack to class, which I think is totally stupid. Teachers say it's because it makes too much of a mess to have backpacks stacked by the classroom doors, but what's even messier is carrying everything around with you from class to class and dumping it all out on the desk when you sit down. I guess I could have used my locker, but that would mean spending a large portion of my day between Misty Marin and Tracy Blair, so I made my way to Miss Garland's class with my stack of books and papers and I tried not to look at anybody.

"Hey, Miriam."

It was Jenny Clarke's voice behind me.

"Hey, Miriam. Wait up."

All around us, on both sides of the hallway, kids walked from their lockers to class, faster now because the early bell was about to ring.

"Come on, Miriam," said Jenny. "I'm just trying to talk to you."

I turned around, slowly. Misty Marin and Tracy Blair were on either side of Jenny. They gave her a little push and stepped back so that it was just Jenny and me. Jenny put her arm around my shoulders. "Hello, Miriam Fisher," Jenny said, reading the words off an index card so that her voice sort of sounded like the voice of an automated telephone answering machine. "Thank you for taking the time to talk with us. Misty and Tracy and myself are making a survey for health class. We would like you to answer a few simple questions for us. Are you willing? Please respond yes or no."

"Okay," I muttered hesitantly.

Jenny smiled back at Misty and Tracy, who were scribbling

things on a clipboard and whispering to each other. "Question number one. How often do you shower?"

I didn't like how Jenny's arm felt around my shoulder, but if I moved away, all my books would fall and then I would have to bend down and pick them up and my hood would slide back and they would see what I had done to my head.

"Every day," I lied.

Jenny turned back to Misty and Tracy. "Did you get that, girls? Miriam says she showers every day." Misty and Tracy scribbled something on their clipboard. "Question number two. What kind of soap do you use?"

"I don't know."

"You don't know what kind of soap you use? What about shampoo? Do you know the name of your shampoo?"

"I don't."

"You don't use shampoo?" Jenny gasped.

"I didn't say that."

Jenny dug her fingernails into my shoulder. "Yes, you did. You said you didn't use any shampoo. We can't change your answer. We're writing in pen."

The early bell rang. Kids started running on either side of us. The hallways were filled with noise.

My heart was pounding. "I have to go to class," I said.

"Just a few more questions. Have you had your period yet?"

She moved in closer. When I didn't answer, she said, "That must be a no." Then she smiled a sick, fake smile. "One more question. Have you ever French-kissed a boy?"

I tried to back up but Jenny backed up with me.

"Have you ever French-kissed a *girl*?"

"She isn't answering," said Misty, scribbling in her notebook. "That must mean yes. Yes for question six."

"No," I whispered. "Stop it."

"No for which question? Period? Boy? Girl? Which one, Miriam?"

I felt like I was going to throw up.

"Answer the questions, Miriam," Jenny said.

"No!" I screamed. "For all of them! No I haven't! Okay?"

The late bell rang. Doors began closing all down the hall.

"You don't have to get so upset," said Jenny.

I turned and pulled my hood close around my ears. Underneath, my mangled hair was hidden from their eyes like one more deformity. I walked as fast as I could to Miss Garland's English class and heard them walking behind me. My footsteps and their footsteps echoed down the corridors, my sneakers and the clatter of their boots. I didn't look back at them when I opened the door to class and let myself in, but I could see rows of kids in front of me watching them and watching me, grinning like they knew something horrible was about to happen.

20

Miss Garland's English class was interminable. The *Oxford English Dictionary* says that *interminable* means "boundless; endless; implying impatience or disgust at the length of something." Sometimes dictionaries are wiser than we know. Jenny and the watermelon girls sat right behind me and I could feel them staring at the back of my hood. Every time I moved they moved. Every time I breathed they breathed. I could hear them cracking their gum and giggling. I sat with a straight back and pulled my hood down over my face and tried to pretend I didn't know they were there. Jenny pressed the toe of her boot into my back. Every time I shifted in my seat I could feel her boot scrape against me, so I tried not to move at all.

I'm not sure what Miss Garland was saying. All I could think about was the sound of gum popping and the boot, and the feeling of the three people I hated most in the world staring at the back of my hood. Sometimes I could focus long enough to nod my head or act like I was understanding, but for the most part, Miss Garland's voice was like the steady hum of a humidifier. It blended in with the fluorescent lights and the buzz of the computers and the other things in the classroom that you wouldn't notice unless you worked at it.

I coughed. Jenny pressed her boot into my back. Tracy Blair and Misty Marin giggled. One of them cleared her throat. A folded-up piece of paper landed on my desk, thrown from behind. I didn't open it. Miss Garland hated it when people passed notes. There was the sound of scribbling and then another folded-up piece of paper came sailing over my head and onto my desk. I didn't open it either.

Miss Garland kept on talking. Sometimes someone would raise his hand. Sometimes Miss Garland would stop and there would be silence. I didn't know what I would do if she called on me. I couldn't think. I couldn't breathe. I kept my eyes on the clock. Twenty more minutes. Fifteen more minutes.

"*Psst*," whispered Jenny.

The toe of Jenny's boot tapped me on the back.

"*Psst*. Miriam. Open the note."

"It's from all of us," Tracy Blair said, giggling.

And then, even though I knew it was a mistake—even though I knew I would regret it forever—I opened the note.

Inside, on crumpled lined paper, was some kind of anatomical sketch of a person who had both male and female parts. They were detailed and they were huge. All the parts were labeled in curvy girly handwriting. And then across the top of the page, in big bubble letters, it said *Freak*.

I clutched the desk with my hands. I squeezed so hard it felt like my fingers were going to break. Behind me, I heard Jenny and

Tracy and Misty giggling. I grabbed the note, crumpled it in my fist, and hurled it at them.

"Ow!" screeched Misty Marin. "Miss Garland, Miriam just threw this at me."

Tracy Blair unfolded the note and held it up for the class to see. "Gross," she said. "Why would you want us to look at something like this? Are you some kind of pervert? Are you trying to make us sick?"

Miss Garland threw up her hands. "I can't believe this. Miriam, what's going on here? You're passing notes? In the middle of *Romeo and Juliet*?"

I didn't say anything. I pulled my hood farther down over my face.

Miss Garland snatched the note from Tracy Blair's hand. "What is this drawing? This is disgusting, Miriam. Why would you draw something like this. Take off that hood. I'm talking to you. Take off that hood and answer my question."

I sat there. Frozen. The class leaned in. Behind me, Jenny removed the toe of her boot from my back. The absence of that pain terrified me. It was like the moment I've always imagined when you are jumping off a cliff or out of an airplane and all of a sudden you are suspended in the air right before the fall, right before you are about to plummet to earth. I sat there with my hood over my eyes and waited for what I knew was about to happen.

Miss Garland reached toward me.

I felt her hand pull my hood back against the bald patches of my scalp. I saw the impossible slow swoop of the classroom leaning forward. The gasp when they realized what I had done. The sound of chairs pushing back against the linoleum floor as kids rose to get a better look. The sound of Tracy Blair and Misty Marin screeching in delight, and then Jenny's voice, low and sharp, *I told you she was a Freak.* Louder than my embarrassment. Louder than the classroom erupting into laughter or Miss Garland screaming for them to get back in their seats or the bell ringing for the end of the period or the sudden swirl of kids all around me laughing and touching my head and high-fiving each other, and then the sounds of sneakers and high heels and the echo of seventh-graders down the hallway, until it was just me, sitting at my desk with my head exposed, and Miss Garland, standing in front of her desk with her hands limp at her sides.

21

During lunch, the cafeteria was buzzing with whispers. Jenny Clarke and the watermelon girls were huddled in a tight circle in the back of the room, and Freddy Harlan and his group were leaning on the tables behind them, watching them look pretty in their tight jeans and their black tank tops. Once in a while, one of the popular girls would raise her face from the circle to glare at my mangled head. I heard someone say "Loser," and then more laughter.

"You want to find a table?" asked Rosie, her voice stiff and strange, as if she didn't know how to make things better.

I followed Rosie to a table in the front. She put her arm around me and helped me sit down.

"Look. There goes Miriam and her girlfriend." Jenny Clarke's voice sailed over the cafeteria.

I pulled Clyde out of my backpack and began writing furiously.

THREAD

What happens when it breaks?
Does it fall to the ground,
slump over like a sack of grain,
spill its insides out on the concrete?
Or does it just hang there
suspended, like an insect caught
in a spider's web?

"Just ignore them, Shakespeare," Rosie said, squeezing my shoulder. "Don't let them get you down. Let Auntie Rosie look at your poor head." She began running her fingers through my torn-up scalp like a chimpanzee grooming its baby. "You know, it's not half-bad. I've got an electric razor at home. If you want, we can go after school and I could even it out. You'd look punk. It'd be cool."

I took my sandwich out of its bag and stared at it. There was no point in eating. I knew I was going to break. I knew I was going to break any minute. I kept my face completely still and tried not to breathe. Rosie kept on smoothing back my mangled head. I could feel her cool fingers across my scalp.

"Hey, Miriam," Jenny called out. "I like your haircut."

Rosie put her hand back on my shoulder. "Miriam. Please. Would you stop writing for a minute and talk to me? The hair will grow back. Everything will go back to normal. Come on. I'll get us some chocolate milk. You wait here. Auntie Rosie will fix everything." Rosie gave me a hug and then started to make her way to the milk line. I watched her go. I watched her red bird's nest get farther away and then disappear.

I took one finger and ran it across Clyde's spiral binding. Suddenly, Jenny was at my elbow. "Is this seat taken?" she asked.

Jenny flopped down into the empty chair. She leaned against my shoulder like we were best friends. "What are you working on? A poem?"

I stared at her.

"You know, when Artie was over at my house, he told me about your stupid notebook. How you go out on the roof to write things down like some kind of deranged lunatic. You should hear the way he talks about you. He thinks you're a real basket case, did you know that? Is that what you write about in your stupid notebook? Do you write about being a basket case? Let me look."

I slammed Clyde's cover shut. My heart was beating in my ears.

"Come on, Miriam. Your admiring public wants to know." Jenny reached over and snatched Clyde from my hands. She started to read.

"Artie's the one person in this world who really understands me. He's going to wake up my poetry. He's going to give me something to really write about. And it all starts today. Today is a scrumptiously serendipitous day. Today is even better than a birthday.

"Wow, you have a really good vocabulary," Jenny said.

Then she ripped the page out of Clyde. She tore it in half. She tore it again and again. The pieces fell to the cafeteria floor like white feathers.

"Let's see what else is in here.

"Sometimes I wonder if there is such a thing as God. Why would there be people in this world as mean as Jenny Clarke, and why would there be sisters who suddenly realize they are beautiful, and then turn their backs, and why would God make adults if none of them ever notice when something is going wrong?

"Proof of God's existence. That's deep. The teachers are right. You are smart."

There was the sound of paper ripping in half and then in half again, the sound of my writing being torn from its bones.

"Oh, I knew you were a pervert," Jenny whispered suddenly. "I knew you were a freaky little pervert. This is the best yet." Jenny stood up with Clyde in her arms and took a breath like she was going to scream my writing out to everyone in the cafeteria. I couldn't move. Maybe it was because I was angry, angrier than I could ever remember being. Maybe it was the eyes of all the kids in the cafeteria, holding me there, fixing me where I was, my mangled head, my body tensed and waiting.

"I am not a human being. I am a lizard. I am under the blankets and I can't stop touching the bald patches I left on my scalp. It feels strange and scary to put my fingers up to my head and feel the smooth of my skin. Lizard cold. Lizard smooth. I thought my life couldn't be worse, but here it is, three o'clock in the morning, and it's worse. It's worse."

Jenny ripped that page out too, and the next and the next and the next until the floor of the cafeteria was covered with pages of

Clyde. I dove to the ground and tried to gather them back up. Jenny just turned and walked away. Then she started laughing.

That's what unhinged me. The sound of her voice laughing at me, her tin-can laughter rising over everything like a tidal wave. It shook me from my roots. And suddenly I could move again.

Here is what I remember about the next few moments:

I lose control of my breath. Suddenly, I am breathing faster and harder than I have ever breathed. I can feel it in my ears, in my head where everything is bottled up. I look around the cafeteria and imagine the popular kids, their faces contorted into bizarre carnival masks. Misty Marin clapping her hands, egging them on. I see her face close up. It takes up the entire room. Her grinning, contorted carnival-mask face, laughing and laughing.

I don't think about it before I do it.

I don't stop and plan it out, or wonder if I'm doing the right thing.

I rip what's left of Clyde out of her hands and slam Jenny Clarke across the face with him, backhanded, so the spiral glances against her cheek.

The popular kids all move forward to watch, their faces crowding in. Jenny grabs me by the front of the shirt and shoves me back over the table, pushing her hands into my flat chest, her fingernails scratching into what would have been breasts if I'd had them.

I can feel her fingernails go in. She grabs Clyde back out of my hands and begins ripping out the remaining pages. *Rip. Rip. Rip. Rip.* In half and in half and in half again until the floor of the cafeteria is littered with torn paper, until there isn't anything left except a spiral binding and a red cardboard cover which she pulls wing from wing and lets fall to the ground. I open my mouth and screech at her, screech at the top of my lungs, not a word, not a name, just a loud, piercing sound.

Then, somehow, Rosie Baker is rushing toward me with a lunch tray filled with food. I take it from her, blindly, while Rosie grabs Jenny Clarke and tries to pull her back. I feel the weight of the tray in my hands. Then I haul back and slam the tray against her. There is food all over the floor. Jenny is slumped onto the green linoleum tile. She lies there and doesn't move.

And that's when I kick her.

Jenny covers her nose and inches away from me.

There is silence in the cafeteria.

I kick her again. There is the sound of whimpering. Jenny curls herself into a ball and turns her entire body away from me, but it doesn't register. She isn't a person. Her pain doesn't matter.

Then, somewhere, far away, in another time, in another world, I hear Rosie's voice and feel her hand on my shoulder, bringing me back. "That's enough, Shakespeare," she says. "We've won."

22

The cafeteria was empty except for me and Miss Garland. I knew they sent her in to talk to me, but I didn't care. The last thing I wanted to do was talk. We sat side by side on the orange cafeteria chairs. I looked down at my lap, and Miss Garland looked at me.

"Miriam," Miss Garland said finally, leaning in beside me. "Please, honey. Tell me what on earth is going on. I'm worried about you. First the note, then the hair, and then this? It just doesn't seem like you."

I looked at the floor. There were remnants of Clyde scattered all over the cafeteria. Bone torn from bone. I reached down and picked up the two red wings of his binding. Then I dropped to the floor on my knees and began to gather his torn pages, shoving everything I could fit into my empty pockets. I hugged his broken binding to my chest and rocked him.

"This has been a bad day for you. People have bad days. But they survive it, Miriam, and whatever is happening, you will survive it too, okay? I don't know what happened, but whatever it is, the grownups can handle it. We are going to help you. All you have to do is tell us what happened, okay? You want to cry, honey? You look like you want to cry."

I ran my fingers up and down the edges of the cardboard.

"You know, Miriam, when a kid like you changes like you did today—when a kid like you starts acting out—teachers assume that something is going wrong in that kid's life. When things are really bad for you, it's important to put your trust in an adult who cares. I care about you, Miriam."

I stared at Miss Garland. She was pretty, but not in the way Jenny's friends were pretty. She didn't wear any makeup at all and she had long hair that went down almost to her waist. None of the other teachers looked like that.

"Miriam, seventh grade is the hardest year. Friendships change. Allegiances shift. I know all about it. One minute you're in love, the next minute you aren't. One minute you're popular, the next minute you aren't. It stinks. Every second of it. Believe me, I know. When I was your age I was just like you."

I counted the bracelets on her arms. Ten. Eleven. Twelve. Thirteen. Fourteen. Fifteen.

"You know, Miriam, I don't want to pressure you, but I'm giving you the chance to tell your side of the story here. You need to know that from Principal Russo's perspective, it doesn't look good. You attacked Jenny Clarke. Every kid in this cafeteria saw you do it. If you don't tell me your side of the story, you're going to be in real trouble. You'll both be suspended. I don't want that to happen to either of you, honey. Especially you. Miriam, Jenny Clarke is in and out of that office every day. It's the only thing in her life she can count on. But I would expect more from someone like you."

They were ridiculous bracelets. Hippie bracelets. Too many colors. Purple and orange don't go together. Even I know that. Sixteen. Seventeen. Eighteen.

"It will go on your permanent record. And that would be such a shame. You're so smart, Miriam. All your teachers love you. You've got talent. You could really make something of yourself. Go to college. Do something with your writing. So I'm giving you a chance here, Miriam. As a soul mate. As a free spirit who recognizes another free spirit. Tell me. What happened this morning that made you so angry? Come on, Miriam. It's time to talk about this."

I looked Miss Garland in the eyes.

"You know, Miriam," she said, "you and Jenny aren't so different."

She took one of my hands between her two and held it. I pulled my hand away.

"Does that surprise you? You think just because you get good grades and she doesn't, that you are so different? Well, I've got news for you, sweetheart. You're more the same than you think. What's happening at home? Does your mother know you're having such a tough time?" She leaned forward. "Do your parents understand you? Do they know what you need?"

I stared at her. Tears came to my eyes, sudden and unbidden.

"I didn't think so," said Miss Garland. "If they did, you wouldn't be in this mess."

23

The waiting room in front of Principal Russo's office smelled like stale fish. I sat on the bench behind the secretary's desk, hugging Clyde's torn pages to my chest. The bulletin board on the wall behind me had the words *Helping Hands* written across the top in bright pink cut-out letters, and there was a poster-sized enlargement of the mayor of our town shaking Principal Russo's hand. On a strip of oak tag underneath the poster, someone had stenciled the words *Come Join the Team* in pink Magic Marker.

Behind the door to the principal's office, I could hear Miss Garland's voice describing what I had done to Jenny Clarke. How she had tried to talk with me in the cafeteria. How I had sat in silence. How she was so worried about me. I could hear her tell Principal Russo that they needed to inform my parents. I could hear her say something about my permanent record. I could hear them mention Jenny's name. Then their voices became lower and more muffled.

When Principal Russo opened the door to let me in, I could see

Jenny in there already and an empty seat next to her. I didn't want to go any closer, but Miss Garland took me by the shoulders and guided me into the room. She sat me down. Jenny didn't turn to look at me, but I got a good look at her face. Her cheek was purple and swollen and there was a scratch across her chin from Clyde's binding. Jenny's skinny shoulders were slumped forward. When she reached up to push a strand of hair away from her bruised face I noticed for the first time that even though she had red polish on her nails, they were all ragged and bitten down to the quick. I turned my face away.

"I am very disappointed in you girls," Principal Russo said. "You know that a fight like this is serious. I have no choice but to suspend both of you. Jenny. You promised me. No more trouble. Now what am I supposed to do?"

Jenny looked down at her lap. I kept looking forward. I knew I should feel something, some remorse or fear or anger, but I didn't feel anything.

"I have tried to contact both of your parents. Miriam, we reached your mother at her studio. She's coming to get you. Jenny, I guess you know we couldn't reach your mother."

Jenny nodded.

"Do you have another number where we can reach her, honey?" Miss Garland asked. "Do you have any idea when she'll be back?"

"I think she's coming back on Monday," Jenny whispered.

Miss Garland and Principal Russo looked at each other.

"Do you have any relatives that live nearby? Any aunts or uncles?"

Jenny shrugged. "Judy usually takes care of me when my mom's away."

"Good enough," said Principal Russo. "We'll contact the high school. You'll sit right here in this office until she comes. I am suspending both of you for one week. And before you set foot in this school again, you had better find some way to make amends. I'm extremely disappointed by your poor judgment. Both of you." Then he turned and stared at Jenny. "You are so much like your mother," he said, shaking his head. "I'll never forget it. She was sitting right here in that exact spot. Too tough for school. Too cool to do homework. She never heard a thing I said to her either. You better watch yourself, young lady. Or you'll end up just like her."

I looked over at Jenny. She sat slumped, defeated, as if the principal's words had hurt her even more than I had.

Miss Garland went back to class. Mr. Russo sat down behind his desk and busied himself with papers and memos. Jenny and I sat side by side on the black vinyl couch and didn't look at each other. The sounds of Carlton Middle School echoed up and down the corridors outside the office. The sounds of sneakers and lockers slamming.

Finally my mother arrived. She and the principal exchanged some words. All the things you would expect a parent to say. How horrified she was, how she certainly did not condone violence in the house, how she would talk to me about my behavior and make sure that nothing like this ever happened again. My mother shook Principal Russo's hand and thanked him. Then she took me by the arm and led me out of Carlton Middle School. We left Jenny holding herself on the black vinyl couch in Principal Russo's office. I watched her disappear over my shoulder as we walked farther and farther away, from the doorway to the hallway to the outside world.

We got into the car. My mother put the key in the ignition and we pulled out of the parking lot. It was strange to be on the street at this time of day. The world had a different quality about it. People looked up from the sidewalk. They watched our car go by. We passed a woman sitting on her porch steps. We passed a barking dog. Then we rounded the corner onto Mill Street and pulled into our driveway. We sat next to each other and looked out at our backyard and the little steps leading up into our kitchen. We sat in our seats and we stared straight ahead and we didn't say anything.

It was my mother who broke the silence. "Miriam," she said, "I know I'm supposed to punish you right now for hitting that girl. I know I'm supposed to tell you that what you did wasn't right. But I can't. You stood up for yourself. And I'm proud of you."

I turned and stared at her. "You shouldn't be," I said.

I unbuckled my seat belt, got out, and slammed the door of the car.

24

An electric razor sounds like the kind of machine that a butcher might use to cut through bone. When you first turn it on, the sound of it shakes you awake the way a dentist's drill makes you bolt upright even before he brings it close to your mouth, before it plunges down into enamel. The buzz of it itches your skin, vibrates the tiniest hairs on your cheeks, the insides of your lips, makes you want to claw your way out of the room; you have to fight with every fiber of your body to make yourself sit still. *Buzz* is the wrong word. *Buzz* is the sound of a happy bumblebee, a fuzzy yellow sound. This was more like the sound of rocks being ground through knife blades, the sound of concrete scraping against iron. This was the sound of a dying man clearing his throat. *Chhhhhhh. Chhhhhhh. Chhhhhhh.*

"Are you sure you know how to use that thing?"

Rosie straightened the towel around my shoulders and smiled at me in the mirror. "Relax. I've shaved my brothers' heads for as long as I can remember. It's easy. You just keep going until the hair is all gone. Are you sure your parents won't freak out?"

"My parents don't care what I do."

Rosie put her chin on the top of my head. I could see her red bird's-nest hair cascading down on top of my mangled face. "You're lucky," she said. "If I was suspended from school my parents would kill me. I wish my parents were more like yours."

"No, you don't," I said.

Rosie looked at our faces in the mirror. "Yeah, I guess you're right."

"Let's not talk about my parents. Just take off my hair, okay? I'm ready to do this."

Rosie started up the razor again. The bathroom was filled with the sound of my hair disappearing altogether. Rosie started from the back below my hairline and buzzed up toward my ears. I could feel the machine against my scalp, carving me, shearing me, evening out the bald patches so that all of my skin was showing, so that my head met the air. I never knew our bathroom window let in such a wonderful breeze.

"You have a cute neck," Rosie said.

"Just concentrate on what you're doing."

Rosie kept going, shaving my head in long strips, keeping the buzz going longer now as she gained confidence. My mousy brown hair fell around the stool like feathers. I could see myself changing in the mirror. With my old hair I had looked frightened and shy. Something about the way the brown, nondescript strands hid my face and my glasses gave my nose too many shadows. Without the hair I looked different. Edges came into view. The line from my chin to my ear. The line from my cheekbone to my temple. The line from my forehead straight down my nose. I couldn't believe it. Was this who I had been underneath? How could I have missed it? I moved my head and looked at my profile. My skin was so white, I could have been made of silk.

"Holy cow," breathed Rosie. "You look amazing."

I rubbed my hand across my scalp. "Yeah," I whispered.

We looked at my face in the mirror. I raised my chin. My face flashed in a way it never had before. I cut the air in a new way every time I moved. I traced my finger from my forehead to the bridge of my nose and across each cheekbone. It was me. It had been me all the time.

"What are you going to do about this?"

I studied my face.

Then I stood up. "I'm going to Judy Clarke's party," I said. "I'm going to show them that they don't scare me anymore."

Rosie put her hands on my shoulders. "I like hearing you talk that way, Shakespeare, but do you think that's wise after what you did to Jenny? You're not going to have any friends there. I mean, they'll all be against you and Artie will be there with Deborah. Are you sure you can handle that right now?"

I rubbed my hand across my smooth, bald scalp and smiled.

25

Before I even entered the Clarkes' house, I could hear the party thundering like a heartbeat into the neighborhood, like a living thing, the notes of a bass guitar, an amplifier turned up, the steady rocking vibration of music and people. Through the window you could see high school students packed inside, leaning against the walls with plastic cups in their hands. Some kids were dancing, some were making out, some were just downing their drinks. The front door opened. Three high school girls, their arms around each other's shoulders, stumbled down the steps and into the grass-bare yard. They had beer bottles in their hands.

I opened the ripped screen door and let myself in.

The music funneled around me. Everyone stared at my bald head as I walked through the room. It was like the parting of the Red Sea. I walked by a couple leaning against a wall and talking to each other. They stopped to look at me. One of them made a comment about my head, but I didn't care. I walked by a circle of high school boys. They couldn't have known who I was. But everyone I passed looked up at me. They stared at my bald head as I made my way across the room. Sometimes they laughed, but I just kept on walking.

I couldn't find Jenny Clarke anywhere. I saw a lot of people I knew: friends of Deborah's, older sisters and brothers of kids from my school. I saw Judy Clarke with her arm around a high school boy. There was a keg of beer in the corner of the kitchen. Kids were pumping the top and spraying beer into plastic cups from a long rubber tube. Sometimes a boy would shout "Shotgun!" and someone would kneel down on the floor and drink straight from the keg.

High school boys looked different from middle school boys. They were bigger. Their hair was longer. They had stubble on their faces and their muscles bulged under their T-shirts. And when they talked, the room resonated with low tones. They clinked beer bottles and leered at girls and lit cigarettes that filled the house with a gray haze.

The other side of the room was lit by flickering candles. There were couples in chairs and on couches, making out. There were couples on the torn Oriental rug. I didn't want to look too hard on that side because I knew if I looked I would find Deborah and Artie, and even though I had acted like I didn't care, I still didn't want to see them with their arms around each other. But as I walked through the room it was hard not to let my eyes look into that candle-lit side, because a part of me wanted to see what it looked like to tangle yourself up in someone else that way. Part of me wanted to study the mouths and the hands and the bodies and memorize what it looked like so that one day when it was my turn I would be ready.

I sat down at a table.

"Do you want a beer?"

I looked up. It was a high school boy. He stood above me with one hand in his pocket and the other holding a plastic cup. I shook my head and smiled.

"What's with the shaved head?"

I didn't say anything. I put my hand in a bowl of chips.

"Hey," said the boy. "You're Deborah Fisher's sister, aren't you?"

"That's right," I said.

"You shouldn't be here," said the boy. "Jenny hates your guts. If she sees you here she's gonna beat the crap out of you."

"Where is Jenny?"

The boy shaded his eyes and looked over into the make-out side of the room. "She's probably in that corner by the couch. That's her regular place. I don't know who she's with tonight. Maybe Joey Mangan. Maybe Buddy Trotsky. Maybe both of them."

"That's disgusting."

"Maybe to you, but Jenny's famous for it," the boy said. "There she is, over there. I was right. She's with a whole bunch of guys."

I looked to where the boy was pointing. In the dim candlelight, I could see what he was talking about. Jenny was leaning against a wall in the corner of the room. She was all done up. Her hair was curled and she was wearing tight jeans and a black tank top and she seemed so small compared to the boys that it made her look like someone's daughter, like some baby doll with grownup breasts in a room filled with men. The high school boys gathered around her, joking with each other, swigging beer, and pounding each other on the back. Sometimes they would push some guy over to Jenny and he would bend her back and kiss her. *One. Two. Three.*

Four. Five. All the other boys in the group dared him to go for longer. Jenny didn't move. She just smiled her red smile and let them all kiss her.

"Stop," I whispered to Jenny, not even realizing until I heard the sound of my own voice that I had spoken out loud.

They leaned her against the wall and took turns.

"Tell them to stop," I said again.

But they didn't stop. And Jenny appeared to grow younger and younger. By nine o'clock she was ten years old, her skinny shoulders pressed back. By nine-fifteen she was seven or eight. She wasn't smiling anymore. She stared past the boys' shoulders, her eyes dull as pennies.

By nine-thirty, the crowd of boys gathered around Jenny had gotten louder and drunker. Some of them tried to get her to drink from plastic cups, pouring beer into her mouth as they kissed her. Then one of the biggest boys pushed her down on the couch and climbed on top of her. He grabbed the front of Jenny's black tank top and tried to raise it over her head. Jenny twisted her body and shouted something at him. She tried to push him off, but she was a baby compared to him. She was barely even there. The boy put one hand over her mouth and the other one under her tank top. He started kissing her again. Jenny's eyes opened wider. She began searching around the room for someone to help her. People must have heard the ruckus. They must have heard the boys cheering, they must have heard the struggle, and they must have heard Jenny's shouting out, but no one moved from what they were doing to help her. They kept drinking their beer. They kept on kissing each other. They kept dancing. Jenny looked wild now. Her eyes darted back and forth across the room, wordless, but louder to me than any other noise in the house.

Which is when she saw me. Which is when her eyes locked on mine and I could see just how tired and terrified she was. I could see that if I didn't help her, no one else was going to. Now I knew what I had to do. I walked across to the darkened room. The music swirled behind me like a funnel and disappeared so it seemed I was walking in silence across the line. I felt my hand along the wall. I found the light switch with my fingertips. I turned it on.

Switch.

Just a tiny movement. And the whole room was bathed in light.

Kids reacted like worms under a magnifying glass. They looked all around to see who had done it. And then the frenzy of buttons and zippers. Of couples reassembling themselves. Brushing their hands through hair. Staring like they had never seen each other before. I walked over to the pile that was Jenny and the high school boy and I grabbed him by the shoulders. With every ounce of my strength I did it. I pulled him off her. I tugged and pulled and pushed and kicked and I did it. I did it. And then I got between them so that he couldn't get back.

"What the hell!" he shouted.

"Jenny," I said.

Jenny looked at me. Her eyes were red.

"What the hell do you think you're doing?" he shouted again.

"Jenny," I said. *"Are you okay?"*

Then Jenny started to cry. It was a cry of fear and shame and it filled the room with the most terrible and terrifying sound.

There was a strange stillness in the room as the kids realized what was happening. Jenny's crying filled up the space. Someone turned the music off. The high school kids started coming over to see who it was. They circled around us. I could see them staring at us. The masses of faces. I imagined what they must have seen: the high school boy pulling himself up from the floor, taking a long swig of beer, trying to save face, trying to look cool; the other boys, the crowd that had been around Jenny all night, moving back into the circle so that no one could tell which ones had been part of it and which ones had not; Jenny Clarke with a bruised face, holding herself on the old crooked couch and rocking, rocking. And they would have seen me. Miriam Fisher. Bald head. Shoulders back. Hands clenched into fists.

"Hey, I know who you are," said the high school boy. He gestured to me with his beer. "You're that freaky kid who's in love with Rosenberg. Hey, you gonna do some Shakespeare for us? I heard you're real good at Shakespeare."

The crowd was silent, looking at me.

The boy took another swig of beer. "Hey, Deborah," he called into the crowd. "You better come here and take your baby sister home. She's ruining the party."

Not a single person laughed.

Deborah and Artie pushed through the crowd. They ran up to me and pulled me toward them.

Jenny sobbed and rocked herself on the threadbare couch. The sound of her voice rose up into all the rooms of the dusty house. It was a chilling sound, the sound of pain and exhaustion and loneliness rising up like the wind that shook the windowpanes behind us. No one moved toward her. They just stood around and looked.

Deborah reached out and took my hand.

"Come on, Shakespeare," said Artie. "Let's get out of here."

26

The late morning sun streamed out from behind Deborah's roof. It lit up the cracked pavement and the red rooftops. It made things look sharper, more in focus: the lines in the bark of the sugar maples, the iron fence, the backs of the cars parked all along the street. I had seen these things a thousand times before. But they looked different today. As if someone had just painted them for the first time. If Clyde had still existed I would have taken him out onto the roof with me, and I would have tried to write a poem about the way sunshine could make an old neighborhood look new again.

Deborah lay back on the roof and shielded her eyes with the back of her arm.

"It's getting cold," she said. "In a few weeks it'll be too cold to come out here."

Artie zipped up his sweatshirt and pulled his hood up over his head. He hugged his knees.

We all sat in silence. We knew that things couldn't be the same.

Deborah and Artie did not apologize. There wasn't anything they could have said. But there was something new. Last night we had walked out of the Clarkes' house together, Deborah on one side of me and Artie on the other. We had walked together back down Old Forge Road and turned onto Mill Street and let ourselves into our sleeping house. Later, we all lay in our own beds, Deborah next door to me, Artie in the attic, and me staring at the ceiling, listening to the triangle of us, the sound of things settling into new places.

Deborah reached out and touched my arm. "You know what?" she said. "You look amazing with your head like that."

The wind blew. Leaves lifted up from the lawns and the sidewalks and swirled in circles above the ground. When I was younger I used to look into swirling leaves and think I could see witches dancing on broomsticks, or fairies, and I would imagine the wind was music, the high-pitched note of a flute.

Artie sat up as if he was going to say something. But then he lay back on the roof, his hands behind his head. I lay back too. I could feel the wind blow across my bald head and the tops of my cheeks and the tops of my hands where I crossed them over myself. I could feel my skin cool to it. Artie breathed next to me. I could see his chest rise and fall, the square of his shoulder moving. I was glad he hadn't said anything. I wanted the silence. It's strange how you can feel the presence of a person even if you aren't looking at them, even if they aren't speaking to you. I could feel myself between Deborah and Artie so clearly I could almost measure the space between my body and theirs without turning my head.

"Miriam," Deborah said.

I didn't look over.

"Miriam."

"What?" I said.

"What you did for Jenny," Deborah said, shaking her head in disbelief. "After what she did to you. I never could have done that. I never would have had the guts."

I closed my eyes. The wind blew across my eyelashes.

"Miriam, are you listening to me?"

"I'm listening," I said.

I could hear Deborah lie back down on the roof beside me.

Then there was the sound of the window opening and my mother leaning out. She stared at all three of us for a moment as though she were trying to remember who we were. She had paint smeared across her cheeks. Her eyes were red. She stared at us and took deep shaking breaths.

"I finished it," she said. "Last night while you all were out. I sat in my studio and I finally finished it. *Child in the Rain*. Brought the shadows in the rain clouds right down. Made the shadows in her face even deeper. Brought out the blue lines in her wrists. Brought out the skin tones."

"I'm happy for you, Mom," I whispered.

My mother smiled and ran a hand through her hair. Then she handed something out the window. "Oh, I almost forgot, I found this package on the back porch a couple of minutes ago. Are any of you expecting something? The girl didn't ring the doorbell or leave a note. Just ran away. Skinny as anything. I don't know why girls these days feel like they have to be so skinny."

I crawled over to the window to take the package. It was wrapped in a paper bag and it smelled like watermelon. I knew who it was from even before I saw her handwriting across the front in purple ink, the letters curving and looping like vines. I would have recognized the handwriting anywhere. *Freak*. A word that looked softer than I ever could have imagined.

I untied the ribbon.

"I know what this is," I whispered, tears suddenly coming to my eyes. And I did know, even before I saw the cover. I could feel it, the weight of the pages, the smooth glide of gold under my finger, the binding, the spine that fit right into my curled palm. It was made of brown leather and it had a cloth ribbon you could use to mark the pages, which were gilded all along the edges so they shone in the sun. I opened it to the first page. There was no writing on it. There was no writing on the next page either. Or the next. Or the next. I strummed my finger across the edge of the empty pages and watched them fan out like the wing of a bird with hundreds of feathers.

"What is it?" my mother asked from inside Deborah's bedroom.

I put the book to my face and took a deep breath. "It's an apology," I said.

Artie reached in his back pocket and handed me a pen. He touched my hand. "Let's leave her alone," he said, and he and Deborah moved away, ducking back into the window, and then the sound of all three of them, my mother and my sister and then Artie himself backing away, leaving me up on the roof by myself with the new book open in my lap to the first clean page. I took the cap off the pen and wrote the first word all in block capitals across the top, each letter bold and dark.

FREAK

REMEMBER

You do it anyway, even if it hurts,
reach back into the attic,
through the smallest opening,
and you look around in there.
I can remember some things
so clearly, I could trick myself,
imagine that I was falling
all over again. The sound of wings,
of feathered voices, whispering.

GO FISH

MARCELLA PIXLEY

©Jill Goldman Photography

What did you want to be when you grew up?

I always wanted to be a writer. For as long as I can remember, I loved telling stories. When I was in preschool and kindergarten, I used to tell stories into a tape recorder. Then once I learned how to write, I began keeping a journal, which I carried with me everywhere I went. I would write down things I saw, things I heard, snatches of conversations, lists of ideas, details from dreams and nightmares. Throughout my childhood, I filled almost thirty journals. I still have most of them in my writing room, spiral bound, leather bound, yellowed, and dog-eared. They are my most treasured possessions. Some of them have even made their way into my stories. In fact, my favorite journal, a spiral-bound notebook named Clyde, is the inspiration for Miriam's journal in *Freak*.

What's your favorite childhood memory?

In the summers, my family used to live right near a tidal river in Gloucester, Massachusetts. I loved low tide, because that is when all the creeping creatures came out, the fiddler crabs that scurried sideways, the hermit crabs, picking their way across the mudflats in their borrowed shells, and if we were lucky, we might even catch a glimpse of the gigantic horseshoe crabs that only emerged on special occasions. If you sat still on the dock, you could watch the wading birds come in to fish for crabs. My favorite was the great blue heron who walked down the river-bed with long, yellow legs, and always seemed to be looking out into the distance.

As a young person, who did you look up to most?

The person I looked up to the most was my Grandpa Sidney. He used to tell me stories about when he was a little boy growing up in Divin, which was a shtetl in Poland. He had nothing but a red cow and a tiny, one-room hut with a grass roof. He told me about how he used to be hungry, and how he would cry to his mother for milk. He also told me about how his father, Jakob, saved up for a long time so the whole family could come to America and start a new life here. My grandfather never had the chance to go to high school or college, but he had natural intelligence. Everything that came out of his mouth was a poem. He had a beautiful lyricism in his voice. And I loved to listen to him. His stories made me want to tell my own. It is the greatest gift any human being has ever given to me. Now that he is gone, it is his voice that I miss most of all.

What was your favorite thing about school?

I loved being part of *Horizons*, the afterschool literary magazine led by my three favorite junior high school teachers. We met once a week after school, and brought our own poetry and short stories to read out loud to each other. We were a quirky bunch of kids. None of us conformed to the rigid structures of popularity that seemed to exist in the 80s. Some of us didn't feather our hair or wear blue eyeliner. Others didn't own the right brand of blue jeans. Some of us watched *Star Trek* religiously. Others memorized words from the dictionary. It was hard to fit in during the school day. But when we were together in *Horizons*, we knew we would be with other kids who would accept our differences. For that hour, we didn't care about being popular. What we cared about was writing. And for that hour, once a week, we were real writers working together.

What were your hobbies as a kid? What are your hobbies now?

Here are some things I loved as a kid: playing the cello, eating lobster (especially with butter and potato chips), pretending to be a unicorn, trying to move objects with my mind, watching *Star Trek*, singing, writing (of course), and playing make-believe games.

Here are some things I love now: writing, reading, walking in the woods behind my house, trying to train my crazy Golden-doodle puppy not to jump all over us, going on insane cross-country car trips with my family from Massachusetts to New Orleans, Minnesota, Wyoming, or Utah, singing at the piano with my kids and my husband, eating sushi, and collecting sea glass and pottery.

What was your first job?

My first real job was as a live animal volunteer at the Boston Museum of Science. Our job was to clean the animals' cages, mix their feed, and handle them so that they became used to human contact. We had screech owls and ferrets, wood ducks and possums. Most of them were animals human beings had tried to keep as pets that ended up being too unruly. My favorite was Hank, the porcupine. You had to wear padded gloves to handle him, and it took bravery because when he was mad, he would bristle. There was also a kinkajou named Honey Bear who had huge, round eyes and a prehensile tail that could wrap around your arm. They called him Honey Bear because he was honey colored, but also because he secreted this strange, sticky substance called "mung" from a gland near his shoulders. It was kind of gross, but I loved having all of this bizarre animal knowledge.

What is on your nightstand now?
A copy of *Autobiography of a Face* by Lucy Grealy
A Passover Haggadah
A gold locket that my Grandpa Sidney gave to my Grandma Dorothy
A cup half filled with tepid chamomile tea
A tattered copy of the Bach Suites for cello

How did you celebrate publishing your first book?
I bought a row of peach trees to plant in the back of the house. Now every August, when the peaches are ripe enough to pick, I think about *Freak* and how glad I am that I never gave up on my dream. It makes the taste of these peaches even sweeter. I think of them as victory peaches. And at the end of the summer, I make peach preserves so that I can taste the sweetness of that dream all year long.

Where do you write your books?
I have a wonderful writing room. My house was built in 1730, and the ceiling in my writing room has raw boards and beams. One beam still has bark on it. Can you imagine how old that bark must be? My writing room is filled with things I like to look at. Things that help me get into the right frame of mind for writing. There is an antique rolltop desk with an embroidered purse and a cameo that my mother gave me one year for my birthday. There is a collection of glass bottles from the woods behind my house. There is an old wooden box filled with letters. There are photographs of my family and a bookshelf filled with journals

and my favorite books. I feel at ease when I am in my writing room. It is one of my favorite places on earth.

What sparked your imagination for *Freak*?

When I was in middle school, my life was very similar to Miriam's life. I was a quirky kid. I knew the names of every *Star Trek* episode. I read the dictionary every morning, and went to school with a brand-new word each day, words like "homunculous" and "cornucopia," which I made sure to use at least three times during the day. This did not endear me to the other kids. Neither did the fact that I wore secondhand clothes and sometimes forgot to brush my hair. Growing up in Newton, Massachusetts, there were lots of girls who were stylish, who knew how to look beautiful, and who were a lot more confident and comfortable than I was. A small group of these girls started teasing me, and by the end of seventh grade, the teasing had become bullying and I started feeling like more and more of an outcast. *Freak* is not a memoir, but it comes from a place of truth. It comes from the feelings that I knew during that complicated time in my life.

What were you like in middle school?

I was a nonconformist. It used to bother me when people tried to follow the crowd: wearing the same clothes, the same makeup, listening to the same music, talking about the same television shows. So I went out of my way to be unique. I listened to classical music. I played Dungeons and Dragons. I kept on playing make-believe games long after most girls had stopped, and in seventh grade, I still had stuffed animals that I played with regularly. One time, I came to school with my hair done up in three ponytails, two on either side, and one on top like a unicorn's horn. The more other students rolled their eyes or made fun of me, the more I separated myself from them, telling myself that they were beneath me because they were not bold enough to be strange. It wasn't until college that I learned how to accept other people, as well as myself. It is okay to fit in. It is also okay to express differences if you want. One important thing I did not understand then is that one person can do both of those things. You can be part of the crowd sometimes and you can stand out sometimes. You can also protect yourself and save your strangeness for the people who you can trust to love and respect you. Human beings are vastly more complicated and more beautiful than I imagined back then.

Did you keep a journal? Do you keep one now?
I have kept journals my entire life, and I continue to keep them. There is something very satisfying about filling a page with writing and then another and then another. I have always loved the experience of looking back at old journals and seeing how I have remained myself even as the years went by. Even though my "voice" changes as I age, and even though I have become an adult with a husband and children of my own, I see myself shining in those journals from when I was a child. I didn't know it then, but writing in a journal has given me a way to talk to myself. The twelve-year-old Marcella can speak to the forty-three-year-old Marcella and tell her she is still a child deep down inside. The forty-three-year-old Marcella can speak to the twelve-year-old Marcella and tell her that everything is going to be okay.

What advice do you have for kids who are bullied?
Don't keep it to yourself. When you are being bullied, you end up feeling isolated and powerless. When you feel powerless, there is a tendency to turn inward, and to separate yourself from others so that you can protect yourself. With whatever energy you still have, tell at least one person that you trust about what is happening to you. Tell another kid in your class, a

teacher, a guidance counselor, a coach, a pastor. Tell your brother or your sister. They can help you feel less lonely and remind you that there are people around that care about who you are. Know that it will get better. The bullying might feel endless right now, but it is not endless. One day, you will look back on this, and it will be a memory.

What challenges do you face in the writing process, and how do you overcome them?

I think the most challenging part of the writing process is making the time to write. Life can get so full, and there are so many things that pull me away from my desk. There is the dog wanting a walk, or a kid wanting a snack, or a stack of student papers that need to be graded. Then the phone rings. I answer a couple of e-mails. I check Facebook. I clean the kitchen. Being a writer means making a decision that there must be downtime during my day when all of those distractions can be pushed away to make time for the story. When I don't give time to the story, it builds up inside me like a sneeze that wants to come out. I become edgy and I snap at people. Then I realize what's wrong. I have been neglecting the story. So I sit and write for a while, and I write and write. And then I can sigh and breathe.

Which of your characters is most like you?

Miriam is most like me. Her voice was my voice when I was in seventh grade, and her problems were my problems. I am still a little bit like Miriam. I still love writing poetry and I still love words. I still have a twisted sense of humor. I still march to the beat of my own drum. I wish I had the confidence as a child as I do now. I wish I could have known that being Miriam was okay. I think it took writing *Freak* to know that for sure.

What do you do on a rainy day?

We have an old, empty barn attached to our house, and on rainy days, the kids and I like to go in there to listen to the sound of the rain on the roof. We once spent a hurricane up there, while the windows rattled and rain lashed above us. At the top of the barn, we have comfy old couches and chairs. There is a rocking horse and a dartboard and a train table and a wooden marble run, and blocks of all sizes. I like to lie on the couch and look up at the ceiling and wonder what went on in this barn a hundred years ago. Rainy days are the perfect days for day-dreaming.

What's the best advice you have ever received about writing?

The best advice I have ever received about writing was given to me when I was in middle school. My teacher knew I wanted to be a "real writer." I wanted to be published some day, and I wanted it so badly that it almost hurt sometimes. I asked him if he thought I would become a real writer one day. I'll never forget what he said. "If you want to be a writer, you will be a writer. All you have to do is keep writing. Be patient with yourself. Never give up." He was right. It wasn't always easy, but he was right. Now, when young writers ask my advice, I give the same words to them. If I can do it, you can do it too.

Tess and Lizzie are sisters, sisters as close as can be, who share a secret world filled with selkies, flying horses, and a girl who can change into a wolf. But while Lizzie outgrows their imaginative play, Tess clings even tighter to her delusions, eventually deciding that living in the real world is no longer an option. Now Lizzie must come to terms with her sister's illness, and learn to let her go.

Read more about Lizzie's journey in

Without Tess

Funeral Lilies

Every Wednesday I bring the battered Pegasus Journal into the high school guidance office. I sit in the rocking chair and lean back so it feels as if the world is holding its breath. I've grown to like this room. I like the painted masks, each one with its own hollow eyes. I like the wooden animals on the bookshelf: the camel, the stork, the wolf raising her face to the moon; but my favorite of all is the wooden horse that hangs from strings above my head. Its mane and tail are made of real hair, and it has red glass mirrors for eyes. It looks into the distance, its dusty head crooked. Tess would have loved this horse. She would have tried to convince me its eyes could cast a spell. I might have believed her when I was a little girl, but now I know better. There's no such thing as magic. *I'll never let you go, Lizzie. No matter what happens to me, I'll never ever let you go.*

I always come five minutes early. I like to sit in the rocking chair and breathe away everything real. Bad grades and teachers who frown when they see me. Letters sent home in sealed envelopes. All the kids who give me distance like I'm some kind of human plague walking the hallway. I breathe away the silence of Isabella Amodeo, who has pitied me for almost five years and who continues to pity me, no matter how much time goes by. That first week, she delivered casseroles to our doorstep: warm food drowned in melted cheese and tomato sauce, meals Mamma could place on the table without looking. I remember sitting down to dinner, staring at the empty chair.

Of course, there were other kindnesses too. Floral arrangements delivered to the door from our teachers, bouquets of white funeral lilies so pungent they made me cross-eyed. I smelled nothing but funeral lilies that whole first month. Even outside the house—even when I was able to get away from the parade of relatives and neighbors, people who would look at me with sad eyes and then turn away—the smell of funeral lilies clung to my skin, my hair, my clothes. The scent was so strong I still smell it sometimes when I think about how it felt to be without her for the first time. So that now, sadness still smells like funeral lilies to me, and strangely, so does the feeling of loneliness, and so does the feeling of relief, because those were all things that I had never known before Tess left me just Lizzie all alone.

Dr. Kaplan walks into the office at 12:35 and sits at his desk. "Okay, kiddo," he says, "just give me a second." He finds my file and mumble-reads his notes from our last session. Then he settles back into his chair and waits for me to open Tess's battered Pegasus Journal.

The whole thing with the Pegasus Journal was his idea. At our very first session, I told him about the journal filled with sketches and poems. I told him how I rescued it from her coffin the day of her funeral and carried it home in the inside pocket of my coat, how I couldn't let them bury it, because I knew that these pages contained the real story of Tess and me and what happened when things changed. Even though I might not want to remember, burying the Pegasus Journal along with Tess would have been criminal. On that first Wednesday, he told me we had no choice. We had to use the Pegasus Journal to help me come to terms with what happened.

"Ready when you are," Kaplan says, smiling.

It's time to start. I open the Pegasus Journal. The pages are fragile, dog-eared, smudged with fingerprints and shadows. Here is a girl with worms in her hand. Here is an army of toads. Here is the profile of a drowning horse. But it is Tess's face that gazes back at me. Tess's eyes and wild red hair. I catch my breath. I remember the day she drew this. How she rubbed in shadows that made the cheek seem three-dimensional, the ears perfectly lobed like funeral lilies. How she used the back of her thumb to bring out the light in each eye so it looked as though the horse was gazing off into the distance somewhere, at a world unraveling, its tangled mane whipping around its face like the tangled hair of a wild girl who doesn't even care enough to comb a hand through the snarls. The horse on the page opens its mouth. It is my sister's voice coming up through the years. *I'll never let you go, Lizzie. No matter what happens to me, I'll never ever let you go.*

FLYING HORSES

W hat kind of wings do you want?"

Tess raises one eyebrow and waits for me to talk. I don't answer right away. She is eleven and I am nine. It is one week before summer vacation. This is a big decision because whatever wings I choose will be on my back for the rest of my life. We are sitting Indian-style beneath our dining room table, surrounded by the familiar legs of Mamma's writing group, the ragtag bunch of grownups who come to our house once a month on a Saturday with their pages and their pens, to drink iced tea, and talk and cry. Here are Mamma's skinny legs with her embroidered sandals. Here are the poet's straight, uncomfortable legs with her high-heeled black boots. Here are the mystery writer's sickly legs covered with scabs and sores. Here are the picture-book writer's old-lady legs, puffy and swollen, with her blue spiderweb veins, and her red potato feet powdered and pushed into loafers.

Tess and I always spend these meetings sitting under the table making plans for our escape. Tess is holding the Pegasus Journal. She has drawn six different sets of wings, each on its own page. Each set of wings costs seventy-five-thousand dollars and fifty-nine cents, but that's okay because Tess is royalty and she keeps real silver coins hidden under her pillow. There are wings made of the following magical substances: water, gumdrops, moonbeams, gold dust, magic feathers, and peanut butter. Only stupid horses choose peanut butter. Peanut butter wings are gooey. They melt in the sun. The stupid horses who choose peanut butter try to fly, but they always fail. They start off just like Merlin taught us—take a running start and then leap up into the sky. *Fly fly, high high, up in the sky, up in the sky.* But the stupid horses end up falling flat on their faces. *Kersplatt.* Talented horses choose moonbeams or feathers brushed with gold dust. Tess tells me I am one of the most promising horses in our class, and I know this must be true because Merlin tells her everything. Tess taps on the Pegasus Journal and looks down her nose at me. She makes a *tick tock tick tock* noise with her tongue to tell me that time is running out.

"I'll have gold-dust feathers," I tell her finally, finding the right page. "I'm a black horse. My mane and tail are gold and I have a gold streak down my nose." I pet my nose with one finger.

Tess pats my bangs, scratches me behind one ear, and picks

up a gold Magic Marker. With one thin hand, she holds my face still. With the other, she draws a line down the bridge of my nose. The Magic Marker feels cool and wet like a tongue.

"Do you have a star or a diamond?"

"A diamond," I tell her, showing her the shape with my fingers. "And I have one gold stocking. On my left front leg. When I trot you can see it flashing and when I canter it's like a golden blur. That's why they call me Sun Dancer."

"Nice to meet you, Sun Dancer." Tess bows her head and I bow back. She colors a gold diamond on my forehead and a gold band around my left wrist. Even though her fingers are skinny-skinny like baby fingers, they are sharp. They dig into my skin and make me want to pull away. Tess puts her elbow down on my arm until I keep it still. "This'll look cool with the gold wings," she assures me. "Merlin thinks you made a good choice. He says he's glad you've come to study with us."

"When will the magic be complete?"

Tess leans forward so she can whisper into my ear. "In about ten minutes," she says. Her breath is too warm on my cheek. The closeness makes me dizzy. "That's when you'll become a Pegasus. I'll get my moonbeam wings a little earlier since I'm older. I'm black with a gray blaze and a gray muzzle. That's why they call me Smoke. I have magical powers. I can see into the future. Plus I can move objects with my mind. Those are powers Merlin taught me. Here. Draw my markings."

Tess closes her eyes and her face gets still and expectant. I take the gray Magic Marker and color a gray stripe down her forehead. Then I color a circle around her nose and mouth. One of the writers says something muffled and the rest of them laugh. There is the sound of chairs shifting, and people shuffling manuscripts. Ice cubes and glasses clinking. "I don't think Mamma's going to like this," I tell her. "She thinks we're playing tic-tac-toe." We look around us at all the grownups' legs. The mystery writer leans forward and scratches a sore underneath her knee. Then she folds her napkin across her lap and smooths out her skirt with the wrinkled palms of her hands. "I don't want to get in trouble. Mamma doesn't like it when we interrupt the group."

Tess grins. "You still don't understand, do you? They don't need to know everything. Besides"—she brings her face even closer to mine—"we're immortal. We don't need parents. Merlin's in charge of us now. Make my muzzle darker. I think you missed a spot. And make sure my blaze is sort of like a triangle." Tess turns to a new page in the Pegasus Journal. Quick as a flash, she scribble-sketches a horse's head. The mane is blowing in the wind and all the different locks are detailed with lines and shadows so you can really imagine the animal staring off into the distance with its fierce, magical eyes shining. Tess colors in the pupil with the edge of her pencil and leaves a white highlight so it looks like the eye is real. Tess hands over the Pegasus Journal and points at the horse that she wants to be.

"You're so good," I say, sighing, tracing the lines of the face with the edge of my pinkie finger. "I wish I could do that."

Tess shrugs and lifts her chin. "Make me a horse," she commands. I darken my lines. I keep the color inside the circle a solid gray. I trace the contours of her mouth without touching the insides of her lips at all. I work slowly until the job is done. Tess keeps her eyes closed. Then she sways a little. She sticks out her tongue and starts making wet, strangled noises like she's going to throw up.

"What's wrong?" I ask.

"The magic," Tess croaks. "The wings. It's happening. It *hurts.*" She rolls herself into a ball. She moves her shoulder blades up and down, wincing and clutching at herself. I can almost see the moonbeam wings coming up from the surface of her back, pushing through the skin, the long, white bones rising like glaciers from the sea, the moonbeams feathering out, each tiny filament, shining, sparkling, until she has wings, beautiful, new, magnificent wings. Tess hunches her back. Then she uncurls, tosses her neck, and whinnies. She turns from one profile to the next, admiring her brand-new moonbeam wings. They are even more special and more magical than Merlin said they would be.

"They are incredible," I breathe.

"I know they're incredible. I can feel them on my back. Lizzie, I need to fly. You've got to get me out of here. If I stay under this table another minute I'll die." Her eyes fill with tears and she begins to shake like the time she had that high fever and Mamma had to put her in a bathtub filled with ice.

"But if we go out, they'll see you."

"Merlin taught me how to turn us invisible." Tess begins to wave her hands in the air.

I grab her skinny wrists. "I think we should stay here until after they're all done with their meeting. If Mamma sees us, she'll make us wash off the Magic Marker. We'll get in trouble."

Tess looks at me, hurt, like I've betrayed her. "It's not Magic Marker," she insists. "I keep telling you. It's magic paint. It's changed me. I'm a Pegasus now. Look at my wings. There's nothing the grownups can do to change me back. After all of your training, after all of your flying lessons, you've got to believe me."

I look at her. She is my sister. She has Mamma's eyes and Daddy's chin and she has gray Magic Marker all over her face. She doesn't have wings growing out of her back. She just has a skinny spine like she's had since I can remember, and shoulder blades that are too sharp for a girl. I look and look at her but I don't see anything. I blink my eyes.

"Don't you believe me, Lizard?" Her eyes are wide. The familiar nickname tugs on my heart and makes me reach out for her. She twines her fingers into mine and looks into my face like she is looking into a mirror.

"Of course I believe you," I mutter.

Tess exhales. I exhale too.

"Let's go," she whispers.

And then I am pulling her out from under the table. We duck between the mystery writer and the poet and we run like our lives depend on it, past the scraggly writers who are drinking their iced tea and looking at their pages over half spectacles and don't see the two invisible horses galloping in bathing suits through the living room, one black with a golden blaze and a golden stocking, the other the color of smoke, with moonbeam wings extending from her shoulders as if she were an angel. They don't see us leap over the coffee table. We link arms and canter together, *one two three, one two three, one two three*, lifting our knees in unison, through the green double screen doors and out onto the long, wooden wraparound porch overlooking the pine needle hill and the tidal river that leads to the nearby ocean. We go down the porch stairs to the hill and take a running start, and then just as I leap with her, my own wings come, my beautiful gold-dust feathers extending from my shoulder blades like sunlight spreading out across the horizon, like beautiful beams of light. It doesn't hurt like Tess said it would. It feels like heaven. We are angels. I will never doubt her again. This is what it means to be immortal. Tess winks at me. She tosses her head and whinnies.